THE
LAST
HAUNTING

BOOKS BY DAWN MERRIMAN

RYLAN FLYNN MYSTERY SERIES
The Spirit Girls
The Shadow Girls
The Whisper House
The Haunted Child
The River Ghost
The Burning Soul

THE LAST HAUNTING

DAWN MERRIMAN

SECOND SKY

Published by Second Sky in 2025

An imprint of Storyfire Ltd.
Carmelite House
50 Victoria Embankment
London EC4Y 0DZ

www.secondskybooks.com

The authorised representative in the EEA is Hachette Ireland
8 Castlecourt Centre
Dublin 15 D15 XTP3
Ireland
(email: info@hbgi.ie)

ISBN: 978-1-80550-042-1
eBook ISBN: 978-1-80550-041-4

*This book is dedicated to my husband, Kevin.
Thank you for always having my back and supporting my work.
Because of you, we have Rylan.*

ONE

CHARLIE LANDRY

Two Years Ago

Leaves crunch behind me, a heavy footstep. I turn in my tree stand and look behind the trunk where I hang twenty feet in the air. The small platform below my feet shifts when I do and my heart races.

I scan the woods, hoping to see a big buck. The rustling was so loud, it's definitely something large. Luckily, there are no bears in this part of Indiana, and the coyotes normally come out at night. A buck is the only thing large enough to make the sound.

Another heavy step crackles through the quiet—the breaking of a branch. This doesn't sound like a deer.

The usual chatter of squirrels stops suddenly. Even the birds no longer twitter.

The hair at the back of my neck tingles and adrenaline pumps in my blood.

Something lurks nearby.

I shift even further in the tree stand and search for the source. The woods wait.

"Hello?" I call.

Branches scratch together above me, creating eerie music that makes my blood run cold.

I suddenly feel exposed way up in the tree and want my feet on solid ground. It's getting late in the morning, and this is a good time to go in.

I sling my hunting rifle over my shoulder and gingerly climb from the tree stand down the narrow rickety ladder. All the while, I continue to search for what might be in the woods with me, but all I see are branches and leaves.

Once my feet hit the ground, I turn a full circle and call hello again.

A squirrel picks up the chatter above me, making me jump but breaking the tension.

"You're being ridiculous," I mutter to myself. "There's nothing out here."

I start up the path toward my truck but hold my rifle in hand just in case I'm jumped by a bobcat or something. Or kick up a big buck.

My palms sweat against the rifle and the leaves crunch under my boots, drowning out the sound of whatever follows me. I quicken my steps toward the truck. I see the blue through the trees and relief flows through me.

A shot rings out and my back near my shoulder burns.

I don't understand what has happened, but my legs crumple and I hit the ground hard. My chest stings and I reach to the pain. Hot blood pours through my fingers, dappling the brown leaves beneath me with red.

I've been shot.

On my knees, I twist to see behind me. Only the woods. The empty woods.

"Who's there?" I shout, panicked, afraid they will shoot again.

The wind blows through the trees and against my face.

I push back to standing and stumble toward my truck. The movement causes more blood to pour from my chest. I can feel it dripping down my back in hot rivulets. I reach the edge of the woods when my strength gives out.

My legs buckle again, and I land face-down on the ground. A branch pokes into my cheek, breaking the skin. I roll onto my side and moan in agony.

"Who are you?" I scream. "Why are you doing this?" My mind races, confused. I squeeze my eyes shut against the pain.

The horrible footsteps begin again, growing closer. I slit an eye open, and a man stands above me. He's dressed head to toe in camo, similar to my outfit, but without the blaze orange for safety.

Even his face is covered in a camo mask. His eyes burn with a fire that scares me as much as the rifle pointed at my head.

"Why?" I croak.

The eyes stare, familiar somehow. They blink slowly, watching me. My own eyes flutter closed, heavy, heavy.

He pushes the toe of his boot against my side, making the pain in my wound ache, hot and intense.

My eyes fly open again and I scream.

He laughs. The laugh as familiar as his eyes.

"Help, you shot me," I gurgle, hoping this is all an accident and he's come to save me.

"I know that," he says. "Isn't it fun?"

My vision grows black around the edges, fades into spots.

I blink hard to stay awake and press my hands desperately to the hole in my chest.

"Help," I repeat as I fade. His fiery eyes are the last thing I see. Familiar but not like I'm used to seeing them.

As I drift away, I finally place the eyes, the man.

His name rolls off my tongue.

. . .

Dark for so long. I float in the darkness so complete it feels like a physical thing. There's nothing with me but the pain.

My eyes flit open, and a different face is above me. A woman dressed in scrubs, her face kind.

"Now don't move," she tells me. "We just got the bleeding stopped."

"Where?" I can barely speak, the effort tearing at my chest and back.

"You're in the hospital," the woman says. "There was an accident and you've been shot."

Not an accident. Not an accident, my mind repeats.

My lips are so dry I can hardly get them to move. "He did this," I whisper.

The woman, a nurse I now realize, stops suddenly. "Who did this?"

I begin to say his name, my dry lips struggling to form the word.

The darkness sucks at me, dragging me down. I fight to surface, to tell the nurse who shot me.

I purse my lips again. Reading my intent, she leans closer, her hair falling on my injured cheek. "Tell me," she says gently.

I say the name.

Then the darkness wins.

TWO

RYLAN FLYNN

Pain tears my abdomen and pulls at my stitches. It hurts almost as much as when I was first stabbed. I'm only halfway down my front walk and Ford's Malibu seems a mile away. Each step makes the pain get worse, but I try not to show it.

When Mickey invited us for brunch, I jumped at the chance to do something. I haven't been out of the house since Ford brought me home from the hospital last week. The walls are starting to feel like a cage, and I need a break from all the boxes.

Another step and I suck in air in pain.

Ford notices my wince. "Are you okay? We don't have to go."

"No, I want to go. Mickey is counting on me," I say as I gingerly take another step toward his car.

Ford opens the car door and helps me into my seat. I slide onto the leather and breathe a sigh of relief.

As we make our way toward Mickey's house, I shift in my seat, trying to get comfortable. Maybe this wasn't such a good idea.

"Are you okay?" Ford asks again, glancing my way.

"You need to stop asking me that," I say with a forced smile. "I can't sit at home anymore. And Mickey said she had something she wanted to tell us."

He reaches for my hand and gives it a squeeze. "Just let me know if it's too much, and we'll go home."

I like that he calls my house home, it makes me feel warm inside. Not for the first time, I wonder if he will continue to stay with me once I'm fully healed from my stab wound.

"You have to stop worrying. I'll be fine."

"How can I not worry? You nearly died, remember?"

"Nearly, but not dead."

"Too close for my taste," he says, taking his hand off mine and gripping the steering wheel.

We drive in silence for a while, the mood tense. Ford has been by my side since I left the hospital. He even took a few days off work to take care of me. It's been both a blessing and a bit of a hindrance. Mom's ghost has been trying to talk to me, but she can't while Ford is there. The little girl ghost, Elsa, that lives with us has been pestering me for attention. I know she's just scared and doesn't understand why I'm hurt. Ford knows Elsa is there, so at least I don't have to hide her like I have to hide Mom's presence. It's all a bit much at home.

This brunch at Mickey's will be a nice diversion.

As we approach the stop sign near Mickey's neighborhood, a small red car suddenly swerves in front of us, cutting us off.

"What in the world?" Ford exclaims, turning the steering wheel hard to avoid the car.

I grip the handle on the door, flinching in pain, as we watch the red car fly through the stop sign straight into a tree.

Ford slams on the brakes and curses.

"Holy flip," I gasp. "Did that car really just drive into a tree?"

We sit in stunned silence at the stop sign for a moment, then

Ford pulls his Malibu to the side of the road and shifts it into park.

"I need to make sure they're okay," he says, climbing out.

Ford rushes to the crumpled red Fiat and pulls the driver's door open. I watch as he leans in, wondering if I should go help too.

Then, I see a man outside the red car.

The way he suddenly appears tells me he's not of this world. Blood stains his face, and the side of his head looks smashed.

He's a ghost.

And only I can see him.

The man clutches his chest and shakes his bloodied head.

As fast as I can with my stitches, I climb from the car and rush to him. "Don't worry," I tell him. "Everything will be okay."

"What happened?" he asks, dazed.

"You were in a wreck. I'm sorry, but you didn't make it," I say as gently as I can.

"I don't feel well," he says. "My chest hurts." He reaches to his bloodied head. "And my head." He suddenly looks at me hard. "Wait, what do you mean I didn't make it?"

I nod toward the car. "Your body is still in there. My boyfriend is trying to save you, but since I can see you out here, you must already be a spirit."

"Spirit?" he asks, staring hard at the car. He steps toward it and looks through the broken windshield. "I'm in there? What happened?"

"You swerved around us, out of control and crashed into the tree. Looks like you hit your head."

He touches the bloody, crushed spot. "Oh," he says absently. "It's my chest that hurts, though. That's why I lost control of the car. I think I'm having a heart attack."

"Maybe," I say, coaxing the words out. "What do you remember?"

"I was on the way back from the gym. I stopped for gas and my coffee. Then I headed home. My chest started feeling tight and I could barely breathe. I guess I lost control of the car." He peers into the windshield again. "I don't understand."

"I'm so sorry."

"What happens now?"

"The light will come for you. You just have to step into it."

I barely get the sentence out before the door of light to the other side opens behind him. He looks over his shoulder at me, terror filling his face.

"You'll be at peace," I tell him. "Just step into it."

His fear fades and he looks away, steps into the light, and disappears.

I wrap myself in my leather jacket, sad to see another soul go, but happy he is now at peace. I turn my attention to Ford.

He leans over the man inside the car, attempting to rouse him. "Stay with me, man. Stay with me," he pleads.

I put my hand on his back. "Ford, he's gone."

"He was awake for a moment," Ford says. "Awake and mumbling. He doesn't want to give up, and I won't either."

I look at the man in the car, making sure he's the same man I saw disappear into the other side. The blood staining his face is the same, as is the head injury. He's gone.

"I saw him cross," I say.

"He can't be gone." Ford pulls back out of the car and stands tall. "I was so close. I really thought I could save him."

Touched by his concern for a stranger, I reach for his hand. "I'm so sorry," I say.

Other drivers have parked behind us, a small crowd gathering around the scene. Ford closes the door on the red Fiat and turns to the onlookers.

"There's nothing we can do now. He's gone," he says.

"How do you know that?" one of the onlookers asks, his face red and flustered. "What do you mean he's gone?"

"We tried to save him," I say to the crowd. "But there is nothing to be done now."

"We have this under control. You all can go now. I appreciate your concern." Ford flashes his badge and the crowd settles down. "I'm going to call this in."

The onlookers disperse to their vehicles leaving Ford and me alone with the car.

"You saw him cross?" Ford asks.

"Yes. First, he told me he was on the way home from the gym and his chest started to hurt. He thinks he had a heart attack or something."

"That doesn't make sense. This man is in wonderful shape. He obviously works out and takes care of himself. There's a gym bag on the front seat and a protein drink in the cup holder. Seems an unlikely candidate for a heart attack."

"He did seem very fit, but that doesn't rule out a heart attack."

Ford rubs his face, clearly deep in thought. "I guess so, but my gut tells me something isn't right here."

"What do you mean? We saw the accident happen. What else could it be?"

"I don't know."

I'm tired and hurting and just want to get back in the car. Before I can suggest it, a police cruiser arrives on the scene. My stomach drops when I see who climbs out of the driver's seat. Officer James Frazier.

As Frazier steps from the car, his shoulders appear stiff. I can tell from his body language that he's not happy to see Ford or me. His eyes fall on me and he shakes his head a little in disgust.

Although he was sweet on me back in early high school, Frazier has since developed a distinct disliking for me. Particularly for my ability to see ghosts and how that sometimes gets me into trouble. Times like this, when I'm at yet another body, really bother him.

"Rylan Flynn," Frazier says. "I see you're at another scene that's a matter for the police."

"Good to see you too," I say, forcing myself to be friendly.

Frazier just shakes his head and turns his attention to Ford. "What have we got here?"

"One-car accident, unfortunately," Ford says. "The car swerved around us, flew through the stop sign, and then drove into this tree. I tried to save him."

I hate the hurt I hear in Ford's voice. Though he's the head detective for the Ashby Police Department and has seen his share of bodies, I know it's never easy. Especially when they die right in front of you.

Frazier walks over to the car and looks through the driver's side window. "You sure you've done everything you can?" he asks.

Ford bristles slightly. "I have. Plus, Rylan said she saw his soul cross over."

Frazier straightens from his inspection of the body. "Oh, Rylan said so," he says sarcastically. "Well, in that case, what are we even doing here?"

"Now, don't start that," Ford says. "We were driving, and this happened in front of us."

Frazier turns away and opens the driver's side door. He presses two fingers to the man's neck, checking for a pulse, then slowly removes them, verifying that the man has indeed passed. Fishing in the man's pocket, he pulls out a wallet, flips it open, and retrieves an ID.

"Jacob McClure," he says. "Looks like he lives just a few blocks from here."

Ford glances at the ID. "Spring Street. That matches what he told Rylan about heading home."

"You know, I can handle this," Frazier says, pulling the ID

away. "It looks like you're not working right now since you're here with Rylan."

"We were headed to brunch at Mickey's, but we can stick around." He straightens his shoulders.

"Seriously, it's just a single-car accident. I can handle it," Frazier replies. "Looks pretty cut and dried." Frazier stares pointedly at me. "You know, I can do police work too."

My side hurts, and I'm in no mood for Frazier's antagonism. This looks pretty straightforward to me as well. The man flew through a stop sign and hit a tree. There's not much else to find out.

"Yeah, maybe we should go," I tell Ford, shifting my feet in discomfort. "Mickey's waiting for us."

Ford looks from me to Frazier, then down at Jacob McClure.

"I don't know," he says.

I'm not used to seeing him at a loss for words, and it's definitely got my attention.

"Is there something else?" I ask.

Ford won't meet my eyes. He looks down at the grass.

"Not really. The whole thing just feels off. But you'll look into this?" He turns to Frazier.

Frazier hitches his thumb into his belt. "You're just looking to make things difficult. The man drove into a tree. What else is there to look into?"

"I don't know. I just get a feeling that something isn't right here," he presses.

Frazier grows impatient with our suspicions. "You two are always looking for a crime where there isn't one. Look, you said Mickey was waiting for you. Just go. I think I can handle a single-car accident. Besides, Marrero's going to be here soon to pick up the body, and you know how he feels about you, Rylan."

I don't like my feud with the local coroner being thrown in my face. If Marrero finds me at another body, I don't know what might happen. I'm not exactly afraid of him, but he is the coroner, and that holds a lot of power.

I hate to say it, but Frazier's right.

"I think we should go," I say to Ford, placing my hand on his arm. "Let's go to Mickey's."

Ford looks at Jacob McClure through the driver's side window. I can tell he's debating something, thinking.

Then he must have reached a decision, because he turns to me and says, "Let's go."

He turns his back on the car and Jacob McClure and returns to the Malibu, his shoulders slumped.

As I settle back into the car, a movement near a bush catches my eye. Did I just see the point of a jester's hat?

When I turn to get a better look, whatever I saw is gone.

THREE
ROLAND THE MARIONETTE

I watch her leave the scene I helped create. The work guided by my hands.

They think I burned to death, but they're all wrong.

I'm here to stay, to destroy. It will take more than fire to ruin me. I love fire, it is my friend.

No one's stopped me for a hundred years, why does she think she can stop me?

It won't end until I take all I want.

Now I have my old helper back, and together we're unstoppable.

FOUR

RYLAN FLYNN

It only takes a few minutes to get to Mickey's driveway. A few minutes full of pain. The stitches in my side burn. I feel exhausted, and we just got here.

Ford parks on the street. I shift in my seat but make no move to open the door.

He sees my discomfort. "You're not up for this, and you know it," he says.

"Yeah, maybe not, but I really wanted to see Mickey."

As if summoned by her name, my best friend, Mickey, appears on the front porch.

I raise a weak hand to the window and wave. Concern washes over her face, and she starts across the yard. I roll down the window as she approaches.

"Are you guys coming in?" she asks, her curly brown hair blowing in the breeze.

I press a hand to my side, feeling my face flush. "I don't think I'm up for this," I admit. "I'm so sorry."

"I totally understand," she says. "You went through an awful lot with the surgery and everything after you were stabbed." She places a hand on her own belly, sympathy clear in her expression. "Trust me, I get it. You don't feel good."

"Rain check?" I ask.

"Of course."

She turns her attention to Ford. "Now, you get her home and back into bed."

"You're the best," I tell Mickey as she backs away from the car.

Ford pulls away from the curb, and I wave goodbye to my best friend, feeling like I failed her.

"Am I a bad friend?" I ask Ford.

"Of course not," he replies, though his voice sounds distracted.

"You're still thinking about the guy in the car, aren't you?" I ask.

"Something just feels off. I know it's silly, but my gut is telling me I need to look into this."

"What's there to look into?" I ask. "We watched the car drive into the tree." I don't want to think about another suspicious death, but I don't want to dismiss Ford's intuition. "I honestly feel that if there was something wrong beyond the obvious, he would have told me before he crossed."

"Maybe," he says, sounding unconvinced.

Our route home takes us past the accident. The coroner's van is parked where our Malibu had been earlier, and I spot the gray-haired Marrero on the scene.

"You're not really going to stop, are you?" I ask as the car slows to a crawl.

"Just for a minute," Ford says, pulling the car to the side of the road.

"Do you mind if I just wait here?" I'm not exactly eager to face Marrero and Frazier again.

Ford shifts the car into park. "I'll only be a minute." He

climbs out without looking back, determination clear in his steps.

I try to make myself comfortable in the front seat, watching as he crosses the road to the wreck. Frazier intercepts him, and I can tell from his stance that he's telling Ford to leave. Then Marrero joins them. I roll down the window so I can hear.

"We don't need a detective on this one," Marrero says.

"I think you might," Ford replies. "Something's fishy."

Even from across the street, I see Marrero sigh heavily. "You detectives are always looking for a crime where there is none." His eyes flick to the car and me. "Oh, I get it," he says. "Rylan Flynn thinks she senses something, so she sends her boyfriend to do her work."

"This has nothing to do with Rylan," Ford says, irritation creeping into his voice. "I just think it's strange that the dying man's last words were about a heart attack when it's obvious he was in such good shape."

"Lots of people have heart attacks and don't know they're going to have them. Even ones in good shape," Marrero counters. "Either way, cause of death was from hitting his head during the accident. Heart problems or no heart problems, it doesn't matter."

"Why don't you go home with your girlfriend and leave the work to the police? You're not even on duty," Frazier says.

"Why don't you let me do my job? Why are you even here? You the only officer we have on duty in this town?"

Frazier steps toward Ford, but Marrero interrupts, "Can we get back to business here, gentlemen?"

Visibly irritated, Ford turns on his heel and stalks back across the street. He climbs in next to me but makes no move to start the car. He just stares as they load Jacob McClure's body into the back of the coroner's van and drive away.

I sit quietly, wishing I had another pain pill.

I understand why he's so upset. I've often been on the other side, thinking something was a crime when no one else did. I know what it's like to butt heads with Marrero and even Officer Frazier. The only difference is that usually I'm the one trying to convince them of a crime, not Ford.

Ford finally turns away from the scene and looks at me. "I'm sorry. I know you're hurting. We should get home."

The burning in my side is all I can think about. "Yeah, I've definitely overdone it," I say.

Ford takes one last glance at the red Fiat wrapped around the tree. "Sorry, Jacob," he whispers, then puts the Malibu in drive.

"Trash goes out tomorrow, doesn't it?" Ford asks as he pulls into my driveway and parks.

"Yeah, I think so," I say, following his train of thought.

Since Ford has been taking care of me, he's also been cleaning out my house. I enjoy the company and appreciate the help. The clutter is so overwhelming, and I hate that I did this to Mom's house.

"I don't know what to do," I had told him once late at night.

"Just one box at a time," he'd said.

He's filled up several bins, and there's a big pile by the garage of stuff to get rid of.

"I think I'll let you take a nap," he says. "And maybe I'll keep working on the dining room."

I don't have the energy to argue, or the inclination. In my heart of hearts, I wish I could go to sleep and wake up to a clear house, the way my mom had it before I moved in. I'm ashamed that Ford even knows about the hoarding, let alone that he's loading boxes and trash out.

He helps me from the car, through the front door, and into the nearly cleared entryway. Soon, I've had my pain pill and I'm settled in bed and ready for a nap. He tucks me in like a child, and I let him.

"Actually, instead of cleaning, I think I might go talk to Tyler," he says, referring to his detective partner.

"You're still thinking about Jacob McClure, aren't you?" I ask.

"Do you think I'm nuts?"

"No. I get it. I really get it. You go do what you need to do."

He kisses me gently on the lips. "I won't be gone long."

Behind him, I see Mom's ghost waiting in the doorway with Elsa, the little girl ghost, close behind her. It's been hard, not being able to talk to them with Ford always around. This is the first time he's left my side.

"Take your time," I call as he leaves the room.

"I thought he'd never leave," Mom says, stepping into my room.

FIVE

RYLAN FLYNN

"That's not nice," I tell Mom. "Ford has been a huge help while I've been recovering."

She waves her hand dismissively. "I know that, but I wanted to talk to you, and I can't while he's here."

I know exactly what this is about, and excitement stirs in my chest. While I was in the hospital, Mom's ghost asked me to help solve her murder. I've always known she was murdered, but until recently, her spirit hadn't realized it. Not until she discovered the hole behind her ear.

"Are you going to catch the bad guy, Rylan?" Elsa asks, sitting on the edge of my bed next to Onyx, the cat.

"I'll do my best," I tell her. "But I need more to go on. I've been trying to figure this out for two years and got nowhere. Do you have any idea who it was, Mom?"

Mom chews on her thumbnail, thinking. "I've given this a lot of consideration, but I really don't like where it's leading me."

"What do you mean?" I ask.

"Yeah, Miss Margie, what's that supposed to mean? Leading

to where?" Elsa asks while trying to pet the cat. Onyx shifts away and meows loudly as if he can sense her.

Mom hesitates, then shrugs one shoulder. "Well, don't they say that women are most likely to be killed by a romantic partner?"

I study her face, confused. "Yes, that's what they say. But you didn't have a romantic partner. You and Dad divorced years before that."

"Oh, Rylan." She sighs, then gives me a look, a smug expression I'm not used to seeing on her face. "You don't know everything about me."

My eyes narrow. "Are you telling me you had a boyfriend I didn't know about?"

"I don't know if I'd call him a *boyfriend* exactly," she says. "That's a word you kids use. But there was a man. He and I spent quite a bit of time together. I can't believe he would hurt me, but statistically speaking, that's usually how it goes. So maybe."

"What's his name?" I ask.

"Yeah, Miss Margie, who was your boyfriend?" Elsa chimes in.

Mom hesitates for only a second before saying, "Jon Holtzberry."

I blink. "Detective Holtzberry?"

She nods.

"I had no idea. Did you know he was a detective on your case? That seems unusual. He should have disclosed your relationship. He wasn't married or anything, was he?" I ask quickly.

"Rylan Flynn, of course not!" she says, sounding offended. "I would never do that. But we did want to keep it between us. It kind of made it more romantic, if that makes sense."

"Yeah, that makes sense, I guess." I sit back against the headboard, trying to absorb the revelation. "I'm just surprised I didn't know. You hid it so well. But beyond the fact that the boyfriend is usually the perpetrator, what makes you think Detective Holtzberry would have hurt you?" I ask.

Elsa tries to pat Onyx again, but the cat jumps off the bed and bolts out of the room, startling us.

"Onyx knows I'm here," Elsa says, obviously having lost interest in the boyfriend discussion.

"Elsa, why don't you go into my room and watch some TV?" Mom suggests. "Maybe Onyx is in there."

Elsa shrugs and leaves the room, calling, "Here, kitty, kitty," as she disappears down the hall.

Mom shakes her head fondly, watching her go. "I didn't think this murder talk was good for her."

I push myself up higher in bed. "What are you trying to tell me?"

Mom sits beside me, but the bed doesn't sag. "I need to know if Jon did this." She points to the spot behind her ear. "I don't know who else would have wanted me dead. To be honest, I don't even know why he would. But it's a start." She looks down at the floor, hesitant.

"There's something you're not telling me," I press.

Mom sighs. "Jon asked me to marry him."

My breath catches. "And you didn't tell me anything? I didn't even know you two were dating." I try not to sound hurt, but it stings. Mom and I have always been close. The idea of her having a secret boyfriend—no, *fiancé*—makes my head spin.

"I wanted to tell you, I really did. But Jon had just gotten divorced and was fighting for custody of his daughter, Brandie. She was twelve at the time, and he wanted full custody. He didn't think it would look good if he was dating again so soon."

"But he still proposed," I say. It comes out more accusatory than I intended.

"Yes," she admits. "It was going to be a long engagement. I

thought it was sweet and romantic. You wouldn't understand. I'd been alone for years after your dad and I split up. I didn't think I would ever love like that again."

I trace the pattern on my bedspread with my finger, my mind racing. "Love?" I ask. "If he loved you, why do you think he may have shot you?"

"Because I broke up with him the day before."

Shock slams into me. "If you loved him, why did you break up?"

"It was silly, really," she says, voice soft with regret. "But I never got the chance to say I was sorry before... you know." She touches the spot behind her ear again. "Anyway, my only thought is that he was mad or out of his mind or something and snuck in while I was asleep."

"And called me away," I murmur.

"What do you mean?"

"That night, I was supposed to come over for dinner. Instead, I got a call about a haunting for the show. But it turned out to be a fake appointment."

Mom's eyes narrow. "Jon called you away?"

"If it was Jon," I say slowly, "that would also explain why my statement about the fake call isn't in your case file."

"You've seen the case file?"

"Not exactly," I admit, "but Ford has. He says that part is missing."

Silence stretches between us as we both process the implications.

"What did you fight about?" I finally ask.

"Like I said, it was silly." She exhales deeply. "I had a patient at the ER, a guy called Charlie Landry, who'd been shot in a hunting accident. Gunshot wound to the chest. Another hunter accidentally shot him. Mistook him for a deer was the official verdict. We did everything we could, but he was barely hanging on. I was attending to him when he briefly woke up. He tried to say something to me. I even bent over to hear better, but I couldn't make it out."

"What did you think he was saying?"

"I thought he was trying to tell me the shooting wasn't an accident. That he wanted to name the person who shot him. I wish more than anything that I had understood what he'd whispered, but it was too slurred, barely more than a breath." Her voice wavers, and she appears to be lost in the memory. "He died right after. There was nothing more we could do for him."

I frown, trying to piece it together. "What does this have to do with Detective Holtzberry?"

"That night, while we were driving back to Jon's place, I told him my suspicions about Charlie Landry's shooting. At first, he listened and seemed to take me seriously. But then he got vague. He said it was probably nothing and I should just forget about it."

"That's kind of odd," I say.

"That's what I thought. I pushed him on it. Said if it was murder and he didn't look into it, then he was basically letting a killer go. That didn't sit too well with him. He got really mad then. Told me to leave the detecting to the detective."

"I've heard that before," I say, trying to lighten the mood.

"I told him to just take me home and he did. I fumed all the way here, and when we pulled into the driveway, I said that if he wasn't going to believe me when I tell him something as important as this, then maybe we weren't made to be together." She pauses and swallows hard. "I didn't let him answer, I just got out of the car. The next day, I wanted to tell him I was sorry, but at the same time I thought that he owed me the apology, so I didn't make the call. That night, I was killed."

I want to reach for her hand, want to comfort her in some way. "I'm so sorry," I say, my voice choked.

"If I hadn't been so stubborn, maybe I'd be alive."

"Or maybe Holtzberry has nothing to do with it."

"Ask him," she says. "I know he's not the detective anymore because Ford and Tyler are, but I'm sure you can find him."

I don't want to tell her. Don't want to upset her any more than she is. She reads the distress on my face. "What?"

"Jon Holtzberry died of a heart attack more than a year ago."

SIX

FORD PIERCE

I hate to leave Rylan alone, even for the hour or so it will take to talk to Tyler. I haven't left her side since I drove her home from the hospital more than a week ago. I couldn't. The horrible feeling I had when I thought I'd lost her was still too fresh in my mind. Some irrational part of me believed that if I stayed with her, I could keep her safe. I even took a few vacation days, something I haven't done since becoming a detective almost two years ago.

Now, though, I'm hurrying back to the office, driven by a crazy idea I can't shake. I can't get Jacob McClure out of my head. I saw the accident happen right in front of me, and I know the crash is what killed him. But what caused it?

I pull into my usual spot at the precinct and scan the parking lot. Tyler's car is exactly where I hoped it would be, four spaces over from mine. I just hope he's not drowning in work, trying to keep up with me not there.

I make my way through the parking lot, my thoughts on the wreck. Something darts between two cars in front of me. I stop, stunned. I want to believe it was a dog, but the shape was wrong.

I think it was the puppet.

We thought it was destroyed in the quarry fire. How can it be in the parking lot?

I hurry to where I saw it, but there's nothing. I look under the cars, searching for tiny feet, but I only see asphalt. Shaking my head, I give up. I must have imagined it.

As I enter the station and walk down the hall toward our office, I hear low female laughter coming from the open door. Peering inside, I see Detective Faith Hudson sitting at my desk, using my computer. She's smiling.

"That's what she told me, I swear," Tyler says from across the desks, grinning. "Michelle is a riot."

They both feel my presence and turn their heads in unison.

"Ford, good to see you," Tyler says.

I can sense a frown on my face that I don't quite understand, so I force it into something friendlier.

Faith jumps from my chair, her long dark braids swinging as she stands. "I'm sorry, I didn't mean to take your seat," she says. "We didn't know you'd be coming in today."

"I thought you were still on leave, taking care of Rylan," Tyler says. "She doing better?"

"She's home resting," I say. Then, looking at Tyler, I add, "Can I talk to you?"

Faith takes the hint. She grabs a folder and nods. "I should get back to my desk anyway. It's good to see you, Ford. Tell Rylan I hope she's doing okay."

I watch her leave, not sure why her presence bothers me so much. Faith has always been a good detective, and she's never done anything against me or Rylan. But something about her just rubs me the wrong way.

"You were saying something about Michelle?" I ask, sliding into my chair. It's still warm and it makes me a bit uncomfortable in my own seat.

Tyler leans back, smirking. "Michelle and I have been going out for the past week or so."

I manage a genuine smile. "I'm glad. You two make a good couple."

Tyler studies me for a second before tilting his head. "But really, what are you doing here? Thought you had the day off."

"Did you hear about that accident this morning?" I ask. "A Fiat that crashed into a tree?"

"No, I've been buried in paperwork. Just because you're not here doesn't mean it stops." He grins, ribbing me.

"Yeah, sorry about that," I say. "But I want to talk to you about this accident. I saw it happen. The car swerved around a stop sign and then slammed into a tree right in front of us."

"Okay," Tyler says, hesitating. "What's the problem?"

"The problem is the driver, Jacob McClure, was clutching his chest and telling Rylan that he thought he was having a heart attack."

Tyler raises an eyebrow. "Rylan was with you?"

"We were headed to Mickey's. She saw his ghost and talked to him."

Tyler exhales, shaking his head. "I've seen you like this before. You think something's up, looking for a crime where there isn't one. Maybe you just miss working and you're tired of playing nursemaid?"

"That's possible," I admit. "But I don't think so. We owe it to Jacob McClure to find out for sure what happened."

Tyler folds his arms. "What does Rylan think?"

I hesitate. "She didn't say much one way or the other. She was in too much pain to really give it proper thought. I just can't help questioning why a man who was in peak physical condition would suddenly have a heart attack?"

"It happens." Tyler leans back in his chair. "What do you want me to do about this? I don't really have time to investigate what sounds like a straightforward auto accident."

"I already talked to Marrero and Frazier, since they were on the scene, and brought up my concerns. They both brushed me off. It's their view he bashed his head in the wreck and that's it." I sigh, running a hand through my hair. "Maybe if you say something, ask for a full autopsy instead of just writing it off as an accident, we'll get some traction."

Tyler considers for a moment, then nods. "I could do that. I'm not sure I'll get any further than you did, but I'll give it a try. To be honest, though, I don't know what you expect to find."

I lean back in my chair and stare up at the ceiling. It feels good to be back in my office. Back with Tyler talking crime. As much as I love taking care of Rylan, maybe he's right and I'm not cut out for being a nurse.

Tyler studies me. "So, how's it going with Rylan?"

"Being with her has been wonderful," I admit. "But it's been hard to watch her in so much pain. She's healing, but today was the first time we left the house and it didn't go too well. She's in bed resting now."

"Just give it time," Tyler says. "She went through a lot."

I suddenly remember thinking I saw the puppet in the parking lot. If he really is back, I need to tell Tyler about it. I don't know how to bring it up, so I just dive in.

"I wasn't sure how to explain this before, so I never said anything," I start. "But I think I just saw it again, and you need to know what's out there."

Tyler had been looking at his computer monitor, but now he focuses back on me. "What are you talking about?" he asks warily.

"This is going to sound crazy... but there's an evil puppet loose in town."

Tyler blinks a few times, staring at me, trying to decide if I'm being serious. "You know, I've heard you say a lot of weird things in the last few months, but this is definitely the strangest. You want to explain?"

"It all started back in high school. Keaton and I were at the dump looking around, and he found this creepy jester marionette. The thing sort of freaked me out, but Keaton liked it, so he brought it home. According to Rylan, the puppet has the ghost of a man inside it, a man called Roland. He killed his wife about a hundred years ago." I pause, waiting for Tyler's reaction.

He just nods slowly. "Okay, a puppet with a ghost inside it. What is this town coming to?"

"Hang on, it gets weirder. When Rylan moved back into her mother's house and sensed the puppet was evil, she locked it in Keaton's room and covered the walls with crosses to keep it inside."

Tyler glances at the open door, stands up, and closes it. "You're not making this up, are you?"

"It's all real. I know it sounds crazy, but it's real. We thought the puppet burned in the fire at the quarry, but I think I just saw him in the parking lot. If he's still around, there could be trouble."

"What sort of trouble?" Tyler asks. "Since you've been gone, we have had a rash of break-ins and vandalism. Even a fire. We thought it might be kids, but there's no evidence of that at the moment."

"Maybe it's the puppet, Roland, behind all these break-ins. Has anything been stolen?"

"No, that's the strange part. Nothing is stolen. It's just houses getting messed up. Food tossed on the floor, dishes broken, that kind of thing. A shed even mysteriously caught fire, but the owners put it out. It's been happening all around town with no pattern we can find."

"Sounds like the perfect activities for a haunted puppet," I say, looking up at the ceiling again.

"This job has gotten really weird lately," Tyler says. "Ghosts and now puppets. Remember when we just had crimes to solve?"

"There's been plenty of those too," I say.

I glance at the clock. I've been gone for more than the hour I intended. I feel so torn between work and my responsibilities to Rylan.

Tyler obviously notices my indecision. "Why don't you get back? You are on vacation, after all. I promise I'll look into the Jacob McClure accident."

I stand up from my desk reluctantly. My computer is still on from when Faith was using it. I switch off the monitor.

"Have you and Faith been working together a lot?" I ask, trying to keep the hurt from my voice.

"Chief McKay has us on these break-ins. We've been pretty busy."

"Interesting," I say, walking toward the door.

"She's just filling in while you're gone," he says.

"I know," I say, feeling foolish. "Maybe I'll come back to work tomorrow."

"Especially if we have a haunted puppet to chase down. Any idea where it might be?"

"If it's as awful as Rylan says it is, it could be anywhere by now."

I leave the office and head to my car, thankful that Tyler took my word on the puppet so easily. We've been through some strange things lately, but this one is the strangest.

Did he accept the idea a little too easily? A niggle of doubt gnaws at the back of my mind. Did he already know about the puppet?

I shove that thought away and shake my head. Now I'm reaching for connections where there aren't any.

I glance around the parking lot, wondering where the puppet has been and if he's truly vandalizing and breaking into houses.

Where could he be and what does he want?

SEVEN

ELSA WHITE

I listen to what Miss Margie told me to do and go back to her room. I'm hoping the cat is in here, but he has disappeared into the stacks of boxes and things. I don't like the way the house is so full. There's no place to play. We just spend all our time in this room, watching TV mostly.

Miss Margie often tells me stories or makes up games to play to pass the time. Her stories are often too babyish for me. I'm ten years old now, after all. My tenth birthday came and went while I was stuck in the Darby bear. No one knew. No cake and no presents. Not even a hug from my mom.

What I would give for that. A hug from my parents.

I used to see them all the time before Mom sold Darby at the garage sale. When I was a spirit in the bear, I could see them whenever they came into my room. They mostly cried when they came. Mom would sit on my bed and smell my pillow as she sobbed. Such a strange thing to do.

Dad didn't come as often and never entered the room. He'd open the door and just look in. He didn't sob like Mom, but his eyes glistened. I knew he missed me.

I feel like I let them both down by losing to the leukemia.

I tried really hard to stay. I just couldn't.

Rylan would say it was just my time. Only God can decide when that is.

I wonder about God sometimes. Where is he? Why did he take me so early just to leave me here in this house? I love Miss Margie and Rylan, but I miss my parents and my old room.

I visit them sometimes. All I have to do is concentrate real hard on them, and poof, I'm back in my old house. I could go visit them now, but I don't. I just lie on the bed and stare at the ceiling fan.

Onyx suddenly jumps up on the bed. He pays me no attention. No matter how hard I try, he rarely knows I'm here.

No one does.

It's lonely.

Onyx curls up on the bed, and I turn on my side next to him, pretending we are snuggling.

Something scratches at the window. At first, I ignore it, thinking it's just the wind. I move closer to the cat. He jumps up and looks at the window, his tail held high.

"What is it?" I ask him, following his gaze.

A tiny wooden hand is knocking on the glass in little taps. I know it's the puppet. "Elsa, I want to be your friend," a voice coos. It's not like the voice I heard before from Roland. He was scary then. Now he sounds sad.

"Go away," I say, but without much force.

"I want to come in. I want to be friends."

Friends. The word is almost foreign to me. Even before I died, I didn't have many friends. I spent most of my time in hospitals or home in bed. I didn't even get to try school for the last two months. I barely remember what a friend feels like.

I scoot across the bed to the window and look out.

Roland is standing on an upturned bucket so he can look directly at me. "Hello," he says, as nice as can be.

"Hello," I say.

"Will you open the window?" he asks, his large red mouth moving up and down. In the sunlight, his jester outfit doesn't look so scary. Even though he is burned and singed, the colors still show. His eyes are surrounded by large blue stars.

"I shouldn't open it," I say, glancing at the open doorway.

"You can, though. I know you're strong enough."

He's right. I can move things basically at will now. Miss Margie and I practice a lot. I'm way better at it than she is.

"I shouldn't," I repeat.

"Don't you want to be friends? We can play." He sounds so nice. Nothing like the evil possessed thing that used to howl in the next room. Maybe he's just lonely. I understand that.

I cross the room to the door, concentrate on it and push it closed.

"That's a good girl," Roland says. "Now come open the window."

I know he can break it. He broke the patio door before.

"I don't want to break it and make a mess. I just want to play with you."

It's like he read my mind. That cinches it.

I concentrate hard and pull the window up.

Two tiny hands slide over the edge, and he pulls himself up. "Help me in?" he asks sweetly.

I reach for the puppet's strings over his head. They are tied to a type of handle that is partly burned. I see where the strings have been retied.

"What happened to your strings?" I ask as I place him down on the floor.

"Don't worry about that," he says absently, looking around the room. "Want to play hide and seek?"

I do.

I really do.

"You go hide," Roland says.

EIGHT
RYLAN FLYNN

Mom's shoulders slump when I tell her about Jon Holtzberry's death.

"He died? I had no idea."

"I'm sorry." I don't know what else to say.

"Here I was, thinking he was happy and alive and out there." She flutters her hand toward the window. "He's dead, like me." She suddenly perks up. "Do you think he is like me? A spirit, I mean?"

The idea is intriguing. Could Jon Holtzberry be a ghost somewhere? I'd love to talk to him about Mom's case.

"The odds are pretty slim," I tell Mom.

"I guess I won't get to see him until I cross. Maybe he's waiting for me on the other side."

I squirm, uncomfortable with the turn this conversation has taken.

Mom takes a deep breath and lets it out slowly.

"I should let you rest," she says. She stands up from the bed and hesitates near the doorway. "Even if Jon is dead, you'll still look into it, right? I need to know if he's the one that hurt me."

"I'll look into it," I say. "At the very least, I can have Ford get me a copy of your file."

She waits as if she's going to say something else, but then just nods and says, "Get some rest," before leaving the room.

I curl onto my side, snuggling into the pillow. After more than a week of just lying around and resting in my bed—on top of the few days I spent in the hospital—all this activity has worn me out. I let my eyes close.

I hear Elsa in the house saying, "Come find me," and I'm happy that she and Mom are playing a game. Not for the first time, I wonder why I keep them here. This house will feel so empty without them. I push those thoughts away and let myself drift into sleep.

I wake to a banging sound. It takes me a moment to realize what it is and where it's coming from.

It's my front door.

I almost never get visitors. Even when I've been home sick these last several days, I haven't let anyone come see me. Aunt Val has asked. Dad has asked. Even Keaton wanted to visit, but I turned them all away.

I want to curl back into my pillow and ignore whoever it is on my front porch, but I know I can't.

I toss the covers off and climb out of bed, happy to see the painkiller is doing its work—my side doesn't hurt as much as it did earlier.

Mom's bedroom door is closed, and I hear Elsa talking behind it as I make my way down the hall. I can't make out the words, but it sounds like she's having fun. I'm surprised Mom is in the mood for games after our discussion about Jon Holtzberry, but the persistent banging on the front door keeps my feet moving.

The dining room is mostly empty now, and the path to the

front door is wider than before. Ford has been very busy clearing out my house, and I appreciate the extra space as I walk through it.

My hand is on the front doorknob when I hear her voice.

"It's Mickey."

I freeze.

What is Mickey doing here? I always go to Mickey's house —she never comes here. It's been an unspoken agreement between us. I don't want her to know about the hoard. It's bad enough Ford knows.

"Rylan," Mickey calls again. "I brought you some soup."

I stand motionless behind the door. I need to open it. I need to let her in. But I'm afraid of what she'll say and what she'll think of me.

"Rylan, come on. Open up. I know you're behind that door."

Busted.

I turn the knob and pull the door open, stepping outside onto the porch. I pull the door closed behind me.

Mickey waits with a bowl of soup wrapped in a towel.

"It's soup," she says. "It'll make you feel better."

I reach for the bowl, but she holds onto it.

"No, it's kind of heavy. Let me take it inside."

Panic swirls in my belly.

She cannot come inside.

"No, no, just give it to me. I'll take it inside and be right back."

Mickey's face softens. "I already know about the hoarding."

My breath catches in my chest, and I feel my face flush.

"I don't know what you mean," I try.

"You don't have to pretend for me, Rylan. I'm your best friend. I've known for a long time."

"How could you possibly have known? You've never been here."

"I stopped by a year or so ago, and you weren't home. I looked in the windows. I saw the boxes, the furniture, all the items piled on top of each other."

I push my hair over my shoulder nervously. I feel like a fool. "You never told me."

"Would you have been happy if I knew? I figured you had your reasons for not telling me."

"I'm working on cleaning it up now."

"Rylan, it really doesn't matter what your house looks like. I came to see you." She lifts the bowl slightly. "Now, would you let me in? This soup is heavy."

I open the door and let her inside, bracing myself for her response. But she makes no mention of the clutter. Instead, she heads straight down the path toward the kitchen and sets the soup on the counter.

"I'm glad to see you're up and around. You didn't look so good earlier."

"I came home and took a nap," I say, sitting on a stool at the kitchen bar.

"How have you been? I mean, honestly, how are you? I know Ford has been taking care of you. I'm glad you two have made up."

So much has happened since Ford and I broke up and then got back together that it seems like a lifetime ago. I suppose, since I nearly died, it *is* like a lifetime ago.

"It's good," I begin to say, but Mickey interrupts me with a scream.

Her eyes are locked on something behind me.

I spin around in my seat.

At the opening of the hallway stands Roland.

He looks even more horrible than the last time I saw him. He's half-burned and charred. One of his hat points is completely missing, seared away in the quarry fire.

Mickey stops screaming and whispers, "Wow. Why is the puppet in your house?"

I'm as surprised as she is.

As far as I knew, Roland was gone. Destroyed.

And now he stands in my dining room, taking small, deliberate steps toward us. Stalking us.

"Hello, Mickey," he says, his voice almost a hiss.

Mickey backs up against the kitchen counter. "Get it away from me. Get it away from me!"

I stand up, stepping between them.

"Roland, get out. Go away."

Then I have an idea.

Maybe I can catch him and make all of this stop now.

I look around for a weapon, something, anything. My eyes land on a roll of duct tape sitting on the counter.

Roland stares at Mickey, hissing her name, terrifying my friend.

I take advantage of his distraction. With one hand, I grab the duct tape, then lunge for the puppet. He jumps sideways, and I get nothing but air. He lands on the cleared dining room table.

"Nice try, Rylan," he says. "It's going to take more than tape to get me."

Mickey inches her way toward the front door. Roland sees her and leaps from the table onto her back.

Mickey screams, clawing at him. I grab him off her and throw him against the wall.

"Run, Mickey!" I shout.

Mickey bolts for the front door and escapes.

Roland gives chase, and I chase after him. We break out into the front yard.

Mickey runs for her car, but Roland is nowhere to be seen.

"Wait, Mickey, wait!" I call after her.

She stops halfway across the yard and turns to face me.

"I can't do this, Rylan. I can't do this with you anymore," she shouts.

I step toward her, my hands out in supplication.

"I'm so sorry. I didn't know he was here."

"That's not the point," she says, shaking her head. "The point is it's dangerous being around you."

I don't like where this is going.

Desperation creeps into my voice. "It's not always going to be like this," I say quickly. "We just need to catch the puppet, and everything will be better."

"Will it?" she asks, her voice quieter now. "I've stuck with you through everything. Heck, sometimes I wished I was the one who saw the ghosts. Not anymore, look where it's led me."

She looks down at the grass, shuffling her feet.

"There's something else going on here," I say cautiously.

She lifts her eyes to meet mine.

"I'm pregnant," she says. "Marco and I are having a baby."

My knees almost buckle in surprise. "A baby?" I echo.

"Yes, a baby. And I can't keep hanging around you, getting attacked by wild puppets, when I'm pregnant with this child."

We stare at each other, breathing heavily.

"Mickey, that's wonderful," I say, taking another step. Our eyes lock, and for a moment, I think she's going to take it all back. Ford's Malibu pulls into the driveway, and the moment shatters.

"Look, I gotta go," Mickey says.

"Wait! Let's talk about this. This is so exciting!"

"There's nothing to talk about, Rylan. Marco and I have already decided." She exhales, looking toward her car. "That's actually why I came over and why I wanted you to come to brunch."

"But what about the show?" I ask desperately.

"You'll have to find yourself another camera person."

"I don't want another camera person! I want you. We've been through everything, Mickey. You can't—"

Ford climbs out of the car, instantly sensing the tension in the front yard.

"What's going on?" he asks cautiously.

"I need to get home," Mickey says, hurrying for her car. "I'll see you around, Rylan."

My heart breaks as I watch her drive away.

NINE

RYLAN FLYNN

Ford watches Mickey's car disappear down the street. "What was that about?" he asks, joining me on the front step.

"She came by to tell me she's pregnant."

"Pregnant? But that's wonderful, isn't it? Why did she seem so mad?"

"She brought me some soup, and I let her in the house." My voice begins to waver. "She saw the house and she didn't care."

"That's good." He puts a hand on my shoulder.

"That part was good, but Roland was here. He attacked her."

Ford's eyes dart to the open front door. "The puppet was here?"

"I don't know how it got in the house, but he jumped on Mickey while she was running away. Then she said," I sniffle, "she said it was too dangerous to be around me. She even wants to quit *Beyond the Dead*." I look at him with pleading in my eyes. "What am I going to do?"

He pulls me against his chest. "This will blow over. She's just upset. The puppet must have been terrifying."

"I don't understand why it is here, or how it got in. Why

would it come back to where I had it locked up? I thought this house would at least be safe."

I hear soft crying behind me. I turn to see Elsa on the front step, sobbing. "I'm sorry, Rylan," she says.

"Elsa is here and she's crying," I tell Ford. "What did you do?" I ask her, my voice harsh. This makes her cry harder.

"I didn't know he would attack Mickey. I'm so sorry."

"You let him in the house? After all I've told you about how dangerous he is?"

"He wanted to be my friend," she sniffles. "I get lonely here."

I look around for Mom. She suddenly appears in the front yard.

"Why's Elsa crying?" Mom asks, full of concern. "What happened?"

I turn on her. "Where were you? I thought you were playing with her. Instead, she was letting the puppet into the house. He attacked Mickey!"

Mom looks completely flustered. "I, I went... well, it doesn't matter where." She hurries over to Elsa and says, "It's okay now. Everything is okay."

For some reason, this infuriates me. "No, Mom, it's not. Nothing is okay. The puppet is on the loose, Mickey just told me I'm too dangerous to be around, and you need me to solve your murder." I stop, breathing hard. "Nothing about this is okay."

Too late, I remember Ford. He's looking at me in shock.

"Who are you talking to?" he asks gently. "Did you say 'Mom'?"

I'm caught. The secret I've kept for over two years is finally coming out. I inhale deeply, barely believing I'm about to tell him.

"Mom's ghost is here," I say.

He rubs his face, distressed. "Her ghost?" He looks around

the yard like he would be able to see her. "Has she been here all this time?"

I don't like the sound of hurt in his voice.

"Yes," I say, feeling small. "Since her death."

Mom and Elsa are quiet, watching. I look to them for help, but Mom just nods encouragingly.

"I thought we were at the point when we could be honest with each other. Plus, I've been sleeping here for over a week, and you didn't think you could tell me about her? Isn't that an important thing to tell me?"

"I haven't told anyone. I wanted to, but I never could say the words. I guess I just liked having her all to myself." My words sound hollow, not enough.

Ford looks out into the street, unable to meet my eyes. "You could have told me. Or at the very least, Keaton. He would probably like to know his mother is still here."

I look at the grass. "I know. I was being selfish."

Ford blows out air in frustration. "Not selfish. Just hurt. I'm trying to understand. I don't know what I'd do if my mom died and was a ghost."

I want to run to him, to grab him and hold on. I can't believe this is going so well. I've been dreading this day for so long, desperate to keep my secret. The dread was worse than the telling.

"I'm sorry."

He finally meets my eyes. "You don't need to be sorry. This isn't about me. It's about your mom and you. I take it she's here now?"

Mom steps up next to him. "She's right by you."

He looks where I motion and says, "Hello, Margie. Glad to see you again."

My heart melts. I don't think I could love him more than I do in this moment.

"Always such a charmer." Mom smiles.

"Tell him about me," Elsa chimes in, her tears gone.

"He already knows about you," I tell her. "He was there when we released you from the bear."

"Oh, yeah." She sounds a bit deflated.

"Elsa wants you to know she's here too," I say, mollifying her.

"Margie and Elsa. Anyone else?" Ford looks around the yard like a crowd of ghosts may be near. He smiles and I appreciate the attempt at humor.

"Just those two. They are plenty, trust me."

"Let's go inside," he says, heading for the front door. "We need to talk about the puppet."

"And about my murder," Mom adds. "Don't forget that."

"Mom wants to talk about her murder too. She thinks Detective Holtzberry might be involved." We enter the house and head to the kitchen.

This makes Ford stop in his tracks. "Holtzberry? How's that?"

"First things first." I remove the cover from Mickey's soup. "Are you hungry? I'm famished."

"Did Mickey bring that?" He takes a seat at the kitchen bar.

"She's a good friend." My voice cracks just a little.

"She'll always be your friend. She's just worried right now. Try not to let it get to you. You know she loves you."

"I know. But a baby will change everything." I spoon soup into bowls and put them in the microwave, thinking. "I'm excited for her, but I don't want to lose her," I admit.

"That's up to you," he says. "Just be her friend and give her a little time. That's all she needs from you."

The microwave dings and I hand Ford a bowl and spoon. We eat in silence for several moments, then Ford says, "Do you want to start with the puppet or with your mom's murder?"

"There's not much we can do about the puppet. I tried to catch him." I spot the roll of duct tape on the floor where I dropped it saving Mickey. "I had some vague plan to duct-tape him so he couldn't get away, but he attacked Mickey instead. For something so small, he sure is wily."

"And also a menace. I talked about the puppet with Tyler this morning, and it sounds like Roland could be tied to a string of break-ins and vandalism."

"What makes you think it's Roland?"

"It might not be him, but whoever is doing it seems to be doing it just for fun. Nothing has been taken, just food thrown around, things broken. That sort of thing sounds exactly like what Roland would be up to."

"No one's been hurt?" I ask anxiously.

"A shed was burned, but the owners put the fire out. As far as I know, no one's been hurt."

"Good."

Mom and Elsa have entered the dining room while we've been talking.

"Is he really that dangerous?" Elsa asks.

"Yes, he is. If he ever comes here again, you must tell me. You can't let him in the house."

"What does he want with me? Why does he want to be my friend if he's dangerous?"

"That's what we're going to try to find out."

"I think that's enough talk of puppets for one day," Mom says. "Come on, Elsa, let's go to our room."

I tell Ford what they said.

"Is that why your mom's room is still clear? Because she lives there?"

I nod. "I could have put things in there, but I had to keep it just the way she remembered. You know, she wasn't always like this. Up until recently, she barely knew where she was or even what she was. I didn't have the heart to tell her she'd been murdered."

"But now she knows, and she wants you to help her."

"She knows, but I don't think she remembers it too clearly. At the time, the coroner said she was shot in her sleep, so it makes sense that she wouldn't remember."

"What's this about Holtzberry?" Ford asks.

"Apparently, they were in a relationship when she was killed. I didn't know anything about it because they wanted to keep it secret. He even asked her to marry him." I shake my head. "Imagine having that kind of relationship and not telling your kids. I'm sure Keaton doesn't know either."

"Why would she think Holtzberry hurt her if they were in love and planning to get married?"

"They had a fight the day before. She thought something was suspicious about a man who died in the ER while she was caring for him. Holtzberry dismissed her concerns, and she got angry. She thought maybe he came back and shot her out of revenge."

"From what I know of Holtzberry, that sounds very unlikely. He was a good man and a good detective." Ford slides his empty bowl away from him. "Who was the man that died in the ER? Why did she think it was suspicious?"

"His name was Charlie Landry," I say. "He tried to tell her who shot him right before he died. She didn't hear what he said. They wrote it off as a hunting accident, but she felt there was more to it."

"I'll have to look into that for you," Ford says. "That brings up something else I want to talk to you about."

I take our empty bowls and put them in the sink. "I'm listening."

"I think I'm going to go back to work tomorrow. Will you be okay without me here?"

"I'm feeling a lot better than I was this morning, so yes, I'll be fine. You want to go work on the Jacob McClure case from this morning, don't you?"

He gives me a half-grin. "Is it that obvious?"

"I'm actually surprised you took off as long as you did, although I'm very grateful. Could you also do me a favor and bring me the case file on Mom's murder? I don't know what I can do about it, but I promised to look into it."

"Are you sure you're up for that?"

"Honestly? No. Especially after what Mickey said about it being dangerous to be around me. Maybe she's right. Maybe I am just a magnet for trouble."

"You've definitely been in some wild scrapes lately," Ford says. "I'd be happy to look into your mom's case again myself. I practically have the file memorized at this point."

"I think it'll take some fresh eyes."

"Don't you think you should just rest some more?"

"To be honest, I'm going a little stir-crazy here. It'll be good to have something to think about besides healing."

"But is chasing down a murderer the best thing for you to do?"

"Mickey doesn't want to do the show anymore, so I don't have that distraction. I can't sit here and stare at all these boxes and things."

"There has to be something safer. Her killer could still be out there and might not like it if they find out you're looking into her case."

"How will they know?" I shrug.

TEN

RYLAN FLYNN

I wake to Ford touching my hair, gently brushing it off my face. I keep my eyes closed, reveling in the moment of peace before the day starts.

His fingers trail away, and I feel a sense of loss when I feel him climb out of bed. I open my eyes and watch him pull on his pants.

"You're up early," I say, wishing he'd come back to bed.

"I want to get a good start on the Jacob McClure case. Tyler texted me a few minutes ago that the autopsy report was in."

I sit up and throw my legs over the side of the bed. It makes my abdomen hurt, but nowhere near as bad as yesterday. "What did it say?" I look for my jeans. I've been wearing sweatpants and pajama pants for days. I think today I'll actually get dressed.

"I don't know. That's why I'm going in now." He pulls his shirt over his head.

"Can you hand me those?" I point to my jeans at the bottom of a pile of clothes on a chair. My room is getting away from me since I've been injured. The pile topples when he pulls them out.

"Boy, I need to clean this room," I say as I wriggle into my skinny jeans. The waist band rubs against my stitches, but it feels good to be dressed.

"I'll help you when I get home." He stops and looks at me for my reaction. "I just called your house home. I hope that's okay."

My heart warms. "Of course it is. Wherever I am, is your home."

The moment gets heavy and our eyes lock. He leans in to kiss me when Elsa calls from the hallway, breaking the mood. "Rylan? Are you up?"

"Yes, Elsa. We're awake. Just give me a minute." I finish dressing as Ford puts on his boots.

"I'm not sure if I'll ever get used to ghosts living with us," he says. "It's a little weird knowing they are both here. Especially since I can't see them. They aren't in the room right now, are they?"

"Not in the room, but Elsa is in the hall."

"You are amazing," he says suddenly. "Taking care of a little girl ghost who's lost."

"God brought her to me in Darby the bear. It's my job to take care of her."

He takes a long moment to answer. "Isn't it your purpose to cross the spirits?"

I don't like the implications of what he's saying, and I fiddle with the sweater I just pulled on. "I will cross her when the time is right," I hedge.

"When will that be?"

"Her mom won't talk to me. I don't know why else she might be here still. I have to figure that out and solve it for her before she can cross."

"Have you tried?"

I haven't and we both know it. "I like having her here," I say. The reason sounds weak. "She's good company for Mom."

"Your mom is a whole other topic. But I have to get to work. We'll talk about it later, okay?"

I don't want to talk about it at all, but I nod and let him kiss me goodbye.

"I think I'll go see Dad this morning," I say, changing the subject and pulling my bedroom door open. Elsa is waiting just on the other side of the door, her lips scrunched together.

"I don't want to cross," she says, pouting.

"You shouldn't listen to conversations through doors," I tell her.

"Don't make me go to the other side," she says. "I'm sorry about the puppet yesterday."

"Don't worry about that now. I'm in no hurry for you to go." She seems pleased by this.

Ford scoots past me in the hall. "I need to get going," he says absently. "Good luck with Elsa and tell your dad I said hello. A visit with him will be good for you, but don't overdo it."

He leaves and I turn my attention to Elsa. "Now, what was so important you had to come wake me up?"

"You were already awake."

"You didn't know that."

She looks at her feet, nervous. "I might have looked through the door. I can walk through doors when I want to now."

I'm surprised at how powerful Elsa is getting. She's able to move things and to pass through them at will. I've rarely seen a ghost that can do both so easily.

"You shouldn't spy on us," I tell her as sternly as I can manage.

"I forgot Ford was in there with you. When is he going to go to his house again?"

This is a question I've wondered about too. I hope it's not for a long time. "I'm not sure. Do you want him to leave?"

She shuffles her feet. "No. I guess not. Although I think I liked it better when it was just the three of us."

"Speaking of the three of us, where's Mom?" I walk to her room and look in. The TV is on, but the room is empty.

"That's what I was coming to tell you. Miss Margie left a long time ago and hasn't come back. I'm worried about her."

"I'm sure she's fine. She leaves sometimes." I try to placate Elsa.

"But not for this long. She left right after you went to bed. She's been gone all night."

My stab wound aches, and I really want my morning pain pill. What I don't want is the added worry of where Mom might be. I go to the kitchen and open the cabinet, hunting for my pills. Elsa watches from the dining area.

"Aren't you going to go look for Miss Margie?"

I down a pill with a sip of water before I answer. "She'll be back. She always comes back." I grab my leather jacket from the chair. The weight of it feels good on my shoulders. I feel almost normal again.

"Are you leaving too?" Elsa asks, an edge of concern in her voice.

"I want to go see my dad," I explain. "He's been calling and wanting to visit, and I can't keep putting him off."

"Why doesn't he just come here?" she asks reasonably.

I motion to the piles. "I don't want him to see the mess I've made," I say honestly.

"But it looks much better now. Ford has been really busy." She nibbles on a fingernail, then asks, "Why do you have so much stuff? I've never seen a house look like this."

"It's hard to explain. Bringing the stuff into the house made me feel good when I was going through a bad time. Then having the things made me feel safer from the ghosts."

"You were afraid of the ghosts?"

"Some of them. Not all ghosts are nice like you and Mom."

"You mean the puppet. You said he had the ghost of a man

that died a long time ago inside him. The man was not nice, right?"

"He wasn't nice at all."

"So, why is he so nice to me? He talked sweet and he played with me. I don't understand."

"I don't understand either. I wish I did. Just stay away from him if he comes again. Don't let him in the house."

"What if he breaks the door again?"

"I don't think he will. If he was going to, he'd have broken it yesterday instead of tricking you."

Elsa's face crumples a bit. "I'm sorry again. I don't know what I was thinking."

"Don't worry about it," I assure her. "Just keep away from him."

I'm itching to get out of the house and visit Dad, but I also don't want to leave Elsa home alone.

Where is Mom?

Onyx runs down the hall into the kitchen, startled. Behind him, Mom walks in.

"There you are," I say. "Where have you been?"

Mom seems surprised at my question. "What do you mean?"

"Elsa said you left last night and have been gone all this time."

"I don't always stay here, you know that. I'm allowed to go where I want." This conversation feels familiar, but our roles are reversed now.

I exhale heavily. "Are you staying home now?"

Mom looks me over. "You're dressed to go out. Where are you going? Are you really up to leaving the house?"

"I'm feeling much better. I want to go see Dad. Can you keep an eye on Elsa?"

"I don't need a babysitter," Elsa protests.

"It's not a babysitter. I just want to make sure you're safe."

"I'm already dead. What else can happen to me?"

This bluntness brings me up short. How do I respond to that?

"Don't talk like that," Mom admonishes. "Let's go read. We have the *Little House on the Prairie* books that Rylan loved as a kid. You can hold the book, and I'll read to you."

"I know how to read," she huffs.

"Elsa, stop being so difficult." Mom uses the voice I remember from childhood. The one that means business.

Elsa looks to me for backup. "Go read the books. They're really good. You'll like them," I tell her.

She hesitates but finally goes with Mom to their room.

Alone in the kitchen, I make myself a to-go coffee. My stitches are not as painful as they were yesterday, and the pain pill is working its magic. A visit to Dad will be a good thing. I don't know how much longer I can keep him from coming here. I'm running out of excuses to keep him away. I'm glad the house is getting cleared because I can't pretend it's okay any longer.

I also want to tell him about Mom's ghost being here. Now that I've told Ford and my secret is out, it's time I tell my family.

I shouldn't have kept the secret so long.

ELEVEN
FORD PIERCE

I expect to see Tyler in our office, but the room is dark when I get there.

Where could he be?

I flip on the light and turn on my computer. The routine feels good. I missed working even though I loved spending the time with Rylan. I hope she'll be okay today and not overdo it.

I debate texting her, checking in. My finger hovers over the screen when Tyler walks in.

"Good, you're here," he says, waving a piece of paper in his hand at me.

I slide the phone back into my pocket. "Is that the autopsy report?"

"What there is of it. I pressed your case for a full report, but this is as far as Marrero would agree to. Said it was wasting his time to do a full work-up on an auto accident. To be honest, I'm surprised he did this much."

"You think I'm off the track on this?"

"I think I trust your gut instincts. Besides, it doesn't hurt to investigate it."

I appreciate my partner's confidence. "Thank you. Now,

what does it say?" I reach for the report and scan to the cause of death. "Myocardial infarction? A heart attack?"

"That's what it says. Manner of death is natural."

I sit back in my chair and read the whole report. "Trauma to the skull, consistent with an auto accident, but not fatal."

"So he hit his head, but that's not what killed him," Tyler confirms.

"Interesting." I read the short report again. "I'd believe he died from head trauma more than a heart attack? Marrero said head trauma at the scene. I'm surprised he changed it."

Tyler studies me for a long moment. "What are you looking for exactly? I'll back you up, but what are your thoughts?"

"I think a man that was in such good shape most likely didn't have a heart attack."

"It happens."

"So does murder."

"Whoa. Now that's a jump. Why murder?"

I don't have a satisfactory answer, so I just shrug.

"Do you think it's possible you want there to be more to this since he died in front of you and since you just went through something similar with Rylan? Accidents do happen. It's a hard thing to accept, but that's the way it is."

He may have a point, but I don't want to admit it just yet. "This has nothing to do with Rylan."

"Doesn't it? You said she talked to him before he crossed and even he said his chest hurt. Life and death are out of our control."

"I know that."

"Rylan is safe now," Tyler says more gently.

"I know that too." I pick up the report again. "But we owe it to Jacob McClure to do all we can for him."

"What would that be?"

"Does he have a family? A wife?"

"I found a wife but no kids. Her name is Jessica. Frazier

gave her the notice about her husband yesterday. Want to ask him if he thought anything was fishy?"

I stand up. "I want to talk to her."

"You're going to stir things up with a recent widow? Do you really think that's a good idea?"

"She'd know if Jacob was having any health issues. It won't hurt to talk to her."

There are several cars parked in the McClure driveway and on the street in front of their house. I start to wonder if I'm doing the right thing. Obviously, Jessica will have company. Most likely family and friends lending their support.

Tyler parks the car and turns to me. "You sure you want to do this?"

Just then, a woman steps out the front door and lights a cigarette. She smokes with one hand and wraps the other arm around herself as if she is cold. Even from here, I can see her shaking.

"I think that's Jessica," Tyler says. "Looks like her driver's license picture at least."

"Let's go talk to her while she's alone."

Jessica is lost in thought, staring at the sidewalk and smoking. She doesn't notice our presence until we are almost next to her. Then she looks up suddenly and jumps.

Her eyes fill with fear, then narrow in suspicion. "You're cops," she says, then takes a long drag on her cigarette.

"Yes, ma'am, we are detectives," Tyler says, and we both show our badges. "I'm Spencer and this is Pierce."

"I don't want to talk to any police. They were already here yesterday and told me what happened. What could you possibly want from me today?" She wraps her arm around herself tighter and her shoulders shake.

"We realize this isn't a great time," Tyler says. "We see you have company." He motions to the cars in the driveway.

"Family and friends come to support me. Maybe you can make them leave. I'd rather be alone." Jessica blows cigarette smoke out slowly. "Jackals, all of them."

"What do you mean by that?" I ask.

"I know you can't tell by this house and this neighborhood, but Jacob had money. Family money. Since we didn't have kids yet, the cousins all hope they will be named in the will."

"Are they?" I ask.

Jessica makes a sound of disgust. "No. Everything went to me. They just want to butter me up now and hope for a handout."

"How much money are we talking?" Tyler asks.

"I'm not sure but a few million at least. He inherited it from his parents when they died a few years ago. We only live here because this is where Jacob lived when he was little, before his dad hit it big in the tech world. He said if it was enough for them then, it was enough for us."

"Did this bother you?" I ask.

"No. Why would it? I love this little house, and Jacob and I are very happy here... I mean were happy here." She finishes her cigarette and adds the butt to a can by the garage. She takes another from her pack and lights it. "What do you detectives want anyway?"

"We are just looking into a few details from Jacob's accident. We got the autopsy report this morning."

"Autopsy? I thought it was an accident. Do they do autopsies for accidents now?"

"In this case, we asked for one."

She stares at us for a long moment. "Why?" she finally asks.

I shift my feet. "I just want to be sure. You see, your husband swerved around my car right before he ran into the tree. I tried to help him, but there was nothing I could do."

"So he died while you were there?"

"Yes. I'm sorry."

She lets this sink in. "You feel responsible and are looking for a reason for his death. Let me tell you, there is no reason that my wonderful husband would be taken so early except that God must hate me."

"God does not hate you. He has a reason for everything," I say, surprising myself.

"Easy for you to say. Are you married, detective?"

"No."

"Girlfriend then?"

"Yes."

"Imagine if she was suddenly plucked from your life. Wouldn't you think God hated you?"

This hits so close to home, it makes my stomach swirl. I did wonder that when Rylan was hovering between this world and the next.

"Mrs. McClure, can you tell us if Jacob had heart trouble?" Tyler saves me with his change of subject.

"That's crazy. If that's what your report says, I say your coroner made a mistake. Jacob went to the gym all the time and was in perfect shape." She holds up her cigarette. "Not like me. I'm not a health nut like him. He was after me to quit smoking and to eat better. Guess it didn't matter in the end."

"So no history of health problems?" I press.

"Jacob was the pillar of health. Imagine, him having a heart attack. I told you God hates me."

The front door opens and a man steps out. "Jessica, everything okay?" he asks, placing a hand on the small of her back.

"Yes, Michael, these are detectives. They had a few questions about Jacob's death."

Michael looks us up and down. "Detectives?" He steps closer to Jessica's side.

"And who are you, exactly?" I ask, not liking the man on sight.

"This is our good friend Michael," Jessica says.

"I'm here to support Jessica." There's a slight note of challenge in his voice. "You didn't tell me why you are here."

"Did you know Jacob was worth a lot of money?" I ask, although perhaps I shouldn't.

Michael straightens his shoulders and looks at Jessica. "Well, I'm sure that doesn't matter now. I think it best if you both leave."

"Where were you yesterday morning?" I ask, not sure why I'm being so hard on this friend.

"I don't understand. I thought he had a car accident," Michael says.

"We're just covering all the bases," Tyler says. "Can you account for your whereabouts at the time of the accident?"

"This is nuts. I was on my way to work. As a matter of fact, I did see Jacob at the gas station and we talked for a few minutes, then we went our separate ways. I went to work, and he headed home."

"Did he seem like he was in distress or sick or in pain?" Tyler asks.

"No. He was fine. Why all these questions?"

"What are you getting at?" Jessica cuts in.

"Nothing. Nothing," Tyler says. "Like we said, just wrapping up."

"You think someone hurt Jacob?" Jessica asks.

"Do you?" I counter. "Who would benefit if he was dead?"

"I think you need to leave," Michael repeats, leading Jessica by the elbow toward the front door. "This interrogation is over."

They go inside and shut the door behind them. I hear the lock slide into place.

"Well, that didn't go so well," Tyler says.

"Didn't it?" I counter, starting back to the car. "We rattled him."

"He might just be grieving."

"More like consoling the grieving widow."

"They did seem pretty chummy."

"Too chummy for my taste. I think we're on to something here." I open the car door.

"You don't thing we're reaching?"

"Where there's that much money, nothing seems like a reach. Jacob's death feels awful convenient."

TWELVE
RYLAN FLYNN

As I drive over to Dad's church, I practice what I should say about Mom. How do I explain to him that I've lived with her ghost all this time and didn't tell anyone? How do I even start that conversation?

I don't have any bright ideas on the drive over, so as I park, I say a quick prayer that God will give me the words and that I'm doing the right thing.

My back tingles like it always does when I come here. The cemetery surrounding the church is often full of spirits trying to get my attention. I keep my head down and ignore them as I walk to the front of the church and up the stone steps.

The heavy wood creaks as I open the door. Somehow the sound both comforts and scares me. When I was a little girl, it was my job to prop the doors open when the weather was nice. Dad thought it was welcoming for the church goers to have the doors open. They'd always creaked like this, and the noise frightened me. I'd felt like the people buried in the cemetery were moaning at me.

Little did I know how right I was.

I pull the massive door closed behind me and take a deep

breath of the church air. Some of the tension I've been carrying dissipates and even the pain in my side lessens a little.

The church is quiet and solemn. Dad must be busy in his office.

I make my way down the little hall toward his door. It's closed, which is unusual. Now that I'm closer, I hear soft voices from the other side.

I raise a hand to knock but hesitate. Who's in there?

For a split second, I wonder if Dad has a secret girlfriend the way Mom had a secret boyfriend. He's been single a long time, but, as far as I know, he's never really dated. Except I thought the same about Mom, and was wrong.

Curious, I put my ear near the door. "Next week, same time," I hear Dad say just on the other side. I pull away as the door opens and a small woman with striking silver hair jumps when she sees me.

"Oh, my. You startled me," she says.

"I'm sorry. I just came to see Pastor Flynn," I reply, stepping back.

"You mean Dad," she says with a smile. "I know who you are, Rylan. Don't you remember me? I taught your Sunday School class. Teresa Grant." She holds out a thin hand for me to shake.

Her name is slightly familiar, but my Sunday School teacher was old. In my memory, she is much older than this woman before me. Can this really be Mrs. Grant?

"Nice to see you again," I say, taking her hand. She smiles and smiles without letting go of my hand and I feel like I should say something else. She suddenly leans near my ear. "I've seen your show. I know some people don't believe, but I do."

"I appreciate that," I say, wishing she'd let go of my hand. It's getting awkward.

"Okay, Teresa. I'll see you on Sunday." Dad comes to my rescue.

Teresa drops my hand, and her smile falters a fraction.

"Right. I'm sure you both want to visit. I'll be going."

I step aside so she can leave and call goodbye down the hall. Once she's gone, Dad ushers me into the office.

"I'm so glad to see you up and about again. I wanted to come visit you at home, but you said no."

"I know. I'm sorry. But Ford was taking good care of me."

"I'm glad you have that man." Dad sits on the green couch he uses for counseling sessions. I'm too anxious to sit now that the time has come to tell him about Mom. He seems to notice this. "Why don't you sit?"

"I want to stand. I've been in bed for a long time. It feels good to be moving around a little."

"As long as you don't overdo it."

"That's what everyone tells me."

"Everyone is right." A silence falls over the office and I begin to pace. Dad just watches me for a long moment, then says, "Want to tell me what has you so on edge?"

I stop pacing and turn to face him. "I need to tell you something," I begin. "And I don't want you to be mad at me."

He straightens on the couch. "I won't be mad. Just tell me." There's an edge of concern in his voice.

"Remember how Mom was shot two years ago?" I try. "Of course you remember. That was stupid. What I'm trying to say... Holy flip, this is hard," I stammer on.

"Rylan, why don't you sit down?"

I take his advice and sink onto the couch next to him. "Okay, here goes. Mom died and we went to her funeral." I swallow, my mouth suddenly dry. "When I got back to her house, I found her in her room."

"Found her? Like her ghost you mean?"

"Yes. Her ghost has been living with me since that night," I blurt out.

Now it's Dad's turn to get up and pace. "Your mother has

been with us all this time and you didn't tell me? Why did you keep it secret? Wait, does Keaton know?"

I feel awful, but I shake my head. "No. I didn't tell anyone. Not until yesterday when Ford found out."

"You told him first?"

"He's been living there. He needed to know."

"Right. Right." Dad continues pacing, then suddenly looks around. "Is she here with us now?"

"No. She's home watching over Elsa."

"Elsa, the little girl we released from the bear?"

"She's been staying with me too."

He suddenly flops into the chair opposite the couch. "You've had a full house."

"You could say that." I think of the stuff stacked everywhere and how he doesn't know about it. That's a revelation for another time, or maybe never. I hope to get it all cleared out before anyone else finds out.

"Why now?" Dad asks. "Why tell me now?"

"She asked for my help. She wants me to find out who shot her."

Dad rubs his chin in thought. "You've tried to find out already, haven't you?"

"I looked into it back when it first happened. And I've asked Ford a few times since he and Spencer took over the case. There really isn't much to follow up on. She was shot in her sleep and that was all we knew. Until now."

His head snaps my way. "Now?"

"Mom told me she thinks she knows who might have done it. It's a long shot, but this person was angry with her the night before, and, well, the significant other is often the killer."

He makes a face. "Who would this significant other be? I didn't know Margie was dating anyone."

"No one knew. She only told me yesterday. She and Jon Holtzberry were pretty serious. He even asked her to marry him. But it had to be hush hush because he was recently divorced and was in a custody battle for his daughter. They didn't think dating Mom would help his case any."

Dad sits back heavily in the chair. "Wow. Engaged? I had no idea."

"Neither did I and I talked to her several times a week." I hear a little hurt in my voice. "Turns out they got in an argument the night before she died, and she broke up with him. She changed her mind but didn't get a chance to tell him that."

"So, maybe he was angry and took it to the extreme? It does happen. But wait... Jon Holtzberry? That was the detective on her case."

"I know. A little too convenient. It makes sense that if he did it, then he could have easily covered it up."

"He talked to me several times after. He seemed genuinely upset about her death, but he never let on that they even knew each other."

"He had the perfect cover," I say, warming to the idea.

"So, how do we prove it and get him arrested?" Dad asks.

"That's where it gets even more tricky. He died not long after Mom did. Heart attack."

Dad jumps from his chair and goes to his desk. "That's right." He checks something on the computer. "Yes, that's what I thought. He's buried here. Over on the east side near those oak trees."

He points out the window. I look outside.

"Do you think his spirit might be here?" I ask. "I'd love to talk to him."

"Let's go find out."

THIRTEEN

RYLAN FLYNN

I hurry down the stone steps of the church with Dad close behind. I keep my head up and my eyes alert now that I know there's a specific spirit I want to see in this cemetery. A few shadowy figures seem to look my way, but they don't take full form.

I search for a man's shape. I vaguely remember what Holtzberry looks like from when he questioned me after Mom's murder. To be honest, that whole time is a blur in my mind. I was so shocked and filled with grief, it was all I could do just to get through the funeral. The detective was a middle-aged man with a big mustache. That's about all I remember, the mustache.

If I'd known he was going to be so important, I would have paid more attention.

We search the headstones near the bench. Most of the cemetery is old, with many of the inscriptions from the 1800s. This section is newer, with the headstones noticeably brighter and cleaner than the others. I find the name Jonathan Dean Holtzberry carved into one.

"I thought this cemetery was full long ago," I say. "How did he get to be here?"

"We opened this section several years back. Some of the old families wanted to be buried with their families that had passed before, so we made room."

"Was that what Holtzberry wanted, do you know?"

"There are a few other stones with that name. Maybe they are relatives. I honestly don't remember. I don't handle that aspect directly. Our deacon of grounds handles it."

I nod and stare at the name and dates on the stone marker. My back tingles, but that's normal for here. I raise my head and look around. One woman spirit is watching us but turns away when I wave at her.

"Jon? Are you here?" I call across the cemetery.

The woman looks at us again, takes a step closer.

"Do you know if this man is here?" I ask the ghost woman. She seems startled but quickly composes herself.

"You are looking for Jon?" she asks.

My heart speeds up. "Yes. Is he here? Is he a spirit too?"

She looks past me, over my shoulder. "He is here, sometimes. He doesn't talk to us much."

I look over my shoulder where her eyes seem to be focused. A man with a full mustache is near the bench. "I talk to you plenty," he grumbles. "What do you want?" he demands of me.

"I'm Rylan Flynn," I say. "I can talk to ghosts."

"I know who you are, Rylan. I wondered how long it would take you to get here."

"I didn't know it was important to find you," I say. "Mom just told me about you two."

His eyes widen in surprise. "Just told you? Do you mean...?"

"She's a ghost just like you."

Holtzberry rubs his mustache in thought. "Really? She's here still, stuck on this side?"

"She's been here, but she's worried that you might have had something to do with her death."

"Me? I loved her. I'd never hurt her."

Holtzberry seems genuinely distressed, but I'm still leery. He did have a secret relationship with Mom and didn't disclose it in the police report, after all.

"If you loved her, why didn't you tell anyone? You shouldn't have been on her case. It's a serious conflict of interest."

"I was fighting for custody of my Brandie. She was twelve at the time and having issues with her mom. She wanted me to keep her full-time. Clara wouldn't give in and used every tactic she could to keep me away from Brandie. If she had found out I was dating someone, then she'd have used that against me."

"Are you sure Clara didn't know about Mom?" I ask, a new idea beginning to form.

He looks across the cemetery, clearly deep in thought. "I don't know for sure. I wondered about it when I was investigating, but I couldn't push the issue too much. I did kind of fish around about where Clara was the night Margie was shot. As far as I could tell, she was home with her new boyfriend. At least that's what Brandie told me at the time."

"She was allowed to date and you weren't?"

"Dennis was the reason we divorced in the first place." He shrugs, obviously uncomfortable.

I fill Dad in on all that Holtzberry has told me. "Is it possible Dennis shot Margie on behalf of Clara, to get back at you?" he asks.

"I thought about that. I have to trust what Brandie said about them all being home together. That's as far as I could go without revealing anything about our relationship. If I did that, I'd have been kicked off the case and I couldn't risk it. Besides, I had a theory, and it has nothing to do with Clara or Dennis."

I tell Dad what he's said. He steps toward where I've been facing, confronting a ghost he can't see. "If you have a theory, why didn't her case get solved?"

Holtzberry spreads his hands wide. "Because I ended up here. Dead."

"You didn't have a heart attack, did you?"

"I'm sure it looked like that, but no, I didn't. I was murdered."

"How do you know?" I ask.

"I was closing in on some things I'd noticed about some suspicious deaths in Ashby. When Margie told me about Charlie Landry dying in the ER and how she didn't believe it was a hunting accident, I was already starting to think something was wrong. I told her to drop it. I didn't want her in danger. Looks like I was right about that. Someone was covering up. Someone close to the case."

"You think someone in the police department was behind the deaths? Behind Mom's death?" I ask. "It doesn't seem likely."

"That's what I thought. But I pulled the report on Charlie Landry and added a note to it about Margie's suspicions. I didn't name her directly, but someone must have figured it out."

I tell Dad what he said, then ask, "Who could that be?"

Holtzberry drops his eyes. "I have no idea. That's as far as I got."

"Who did you tell about this?"

"No one. I just started looking into past cases that I thought might have been tied to Margie's or Charlie's. There has been a lot of strange deaths in Ashby. It just seemed to be getting worse and worse over the last few years."

"What are you saying?" I push.

"I think there is a serial killer among us. I think he shot Margie and staged my death among others."

A silence falls over the cemetery. Even the birds are quiet.

"Who do you think it is?" I finally ask.

His shoulders slump. "Someone that knows I was looking into all those previous deaths."

"Who would be able to tell that?"

"Anyone with access to the computer system could see who logged into the files."

"That's a long list. You have to have some idea."

"James Frazier was my leading suspect. He was on the scene at nearly every death I looked into."

Not Frazier. He's grouchy and downright rude, but I can't see him as a killer.

Or could I?

He was on the scene awfully fast yesterday. Did he set up Jacob McClure somehow, then show up to see his work? Maybe Ford was right about it not being an accident.

I don't want to think that of a guy I've known most of my life, but it is possible.

FOURTEEN
FORD PIERCE

Tyler and I only make it halfway down the hall toward our office when Chief McKay stops us.

"Both of you, in my office," he says gruffly.

Tyler and I exchange looks before following him. We stand just inside the door. My back is tense. I have a pretty good idea of where this is going. Jessica McClure must have complained about our visit.

McKay lowers himself into his chair and temples his fingers together over his chest. He lets us squirm, not saying anything. It's a tactic we use when interrogating. Let the silence stretch and the guilty will start talking.

Since I'm the more guilty of the two of us, I open my mouth first. "Is this about the McClure case?"

McKay drops his hands to his desk. "There is no McClure case," he says flatly. "Want to tell me why you were out harassing a new widow?"

He makes it sound so horrible. "We weren't harassing her; we were just asking a few questions. I feel very strongly that there is more to Jacob's death than a simple car accident."

"It was a heart attack," McKay corrects me. "Sounds simple enough."

"There are things that can be given to a person that will make it look like a heart attack on autopsy."

"You've been watching too much *Dateline*," McKay says. "You're looking for trouble where there isn't any."

I'm growing frustrated and can't meet his eyes. Instead, I stare at a photograph on a shelf behind him. It's the chief with some friends, all dressed in camo and blaze orange. A dead deer lies in front of them.

"You've told us before to trust our gut instincts," Tyler says. "That's what we are doing."

"You think this is murder? Mrs. McClure said you basically accused her of it."

"We didn't accuse her. We just mentioned some curious things," I say.

"Same difference to her." McKay shrugs.

"There are things that look bad. Like, did you know Jacob had inherited a lot of money? He chose to live in a modest house and still went to work, but he was worth at least a million according to Jessica," Tyler says.

"And there's the friend, Michael. He talked to us this morning. He seemed awfully chummy with Jessica. Maybe they're having an affair, and he killed Jacob. He said he saw him at the gas station just before the accident. He could have slipped him something?" I suggest.

McKay's neck starts turning a red that soon climbs to his cheeks, a sure sign he's growing angry. "Now that's a stretch, even for you."

I won't back down, even though I know I should. "Is it? It could have happened like that."

"Or Santa Claus could have killed him," McKay says sarcastically. "Look, stay away from this. It's your first day back and there is plenty of work to catch up on. Did Spencer tell you about the break-ins all over town? We have enough to do dealing with that. Find out who the vandal is and then you can go chasing after imaginary murderers."

I already know who's likely behind the break-ins, but I'm not about to tell Chief about a possessed puppet.

McKay waves his hand at the door. "Dismissed."

Tyler hurries from the room, but I hesitate, wanting to press my case. The stern look on his reddened face makes me think twice. Maybe everyone is right and I'm looking for something that just isn't there.

"Close the door behind you," McKay says. I leave the room, and the door clicks behind me with a finality I don't like.

"Guess that's case closed for McClure," I grumble.

Detective Faith Hudson is already in our office when we return. "I might have a lead on the break-ins," she says. "Someone saw a very short person running across their back-yard. We may be looking for a child or a little person."

Thoughts of car crashes and heart attacks are pushed out by Roland. I have to tell Faith about him. It's only fair she has all the details on the cases she's working so hard on. Her past response to ghosts and Rylan have not all been favorable, so I doubt she'll believe this wild story.

Still, she deserves to know.

"Hudson," I say, interrupting her. "We think we know who's behind the break-ins."

She shuts the folder she was looking at. "Would have been nice if you'd told me before," she retorts.

"You'll want to sit down for this," Tyler says, shutting the door.

Faith pulls up an extra chair. "Tell me what's going on," she says. "Let me guess. This is about ghosts, isn't it?"

Hudson really is a good detective to have figured that out already.

"Let me start at the beginning," I say. "When I was a

teenager, Keaton Flynn and I were snooping around the dump when he found a marionette..."

FIFTEEN

RYLAN FLYNN

"That's all I know. Now take me to see Margie. I've missed her and thought I'd have to get to heaven before I'd talk to her again," Holtzberry says. "I've had nothing to do but think about murder since I found myself in this cemetery. I want to see something positive for a change."

"You never thought to go see her before? Or at least the house where she lived?"

"I went once, but it wasn't at all like it was when she lived there. Full of boxes and crowded with stuff. Margie would never have lived like that."

My heart skips a beat and I'm glad Dad can only hear my half of the conversation. I'm definitely not ready to talk about my hoarding today. The revelation about Mom's ghost is plenty.

I direct my words to Dad. "He wants to see Mom. I think I'll take him there now."

"I'll go with you," he says, turning toward the church. "Just let me grab my keys."

"No," I say too quickly.

He stops and studies me. "Is there a reason you don't want me at the house? Anytime I've stopped by you make me stay outside. This last week you wouldn't let me visit you while you were recovering. Now you don't want me to come. Something is wrong."

"Nothing's wrong." I feel awful. I'm lying to Dad at his church. This feels like a new low. "I didn't want you to come by before because Mom was there. And you're busy now—you need to work." It sounds lame and I know it. "There's really nothing you can do. You can't see Mom and you can't see Holtzberry. Plus, they were a couple. Do you really want to be there when they're reunited?"

"I just want your mom to be happy, even if she has passed away from her earthly life. Maybe you're right, though. She won't want to be reunited with him while I'm watching."

My shoulders relax, and I give him a hug goodbye. "Thank you, Dad. I'll keep you posted."

He hesitates. "Tell her I wish her well and that I'm sorry she is stuck here and not in heaven. I'm surprised you haven't tried to cross her yet."

"I did. It wasn't time." Another lie, but easier than explaining why I haven't. Is it so wrong to want my mom with me?

"Can we go now?" Holtzberry interrupts. "If you want to stand here and talk all day, I can go without you."

"I'm coming," I say and wave to Dad. He watches as I drive away, Holtzberry in the front seat.

"The cluttered house is your mess, isn't it? Your dad doesn't know."

"He doesn't and I'd like to keep it that way," I say stiffly.

"All I care about is Margie. You want to trash the house, that's your problem."

"I see dying didn't make you soft," I reply, a little stung by his words.

"Sorry. I guess I'm out of practice with talking to the living. You know, I've seen you at the church before several times. I tried to get your attention, but you always ignore the spirits there."

"Cemeteries can be problematic for someone like me. Better to keep my head down and keep moving."

"I get that." He looks out the window. "So, Margie is still here," he muses. "I could have been with her all this time."

"I didn't know."

"Don't worry about it. We'll be together soon. Death can be lonely, but those days are over now."

We drive in silence until we reach my driveway. "Ready?" I turn to look at him.

"Take me to her."

"By the way, I also have a little girl ghost living here. Her name is Elsa."

"A full house," he says, like my dad had earlier.

"And my boyfriend has been staying here taking care of me. You know him. He became detective after you passed away."

"You're dating Tyler Spencer?"

"No. Ford Pierce. They're both detectives now."

"Ahh, Pierce. Good man."

I warm at the praise. "He is."

"Hope he doesn't mind another ghost living here. If Margie will have me, I won't leave her side again." He gets out of the car and rushes to the front door. I hurry alongside him and unlock it.

He walks right in calling, "Margie? Margie, are you here?" He stops in the dining room as Mom comes down the hall.

"What in the world?" she says, breathless. "Jon?"

"It's me," he says. "I didn't know you were still on this side, but here we both are."

Mom looks to me, a little apprehensive. "He didn't hurt you. He only tried to protect you," I reassure her.

She visibly relaxes. "You did?"

"All I wanted to do is keep you safe, but I failed. But we can get into that later. I'm just so glad to see you again."

The gruff man from the car is gone. Even his voice is softer, lower.

Mom fairly glows. "I missed you," she says.

"You won't have to miss me anymore." He reaches for her and pulls her into his arms.

Mom starts to cry. "I thought... I thought you... I'm so sorry."

"Rylan told me. You thought I was the one who shot you. That had to be a horrible thing to think about." He kisses her on the forehead. "I'm here now. We're together."

"Who's this?" Elsa asks, coming into the dining room.

Holtzberry pulls back and smiles at Elsa. "You must be Elsa."

"You're a ghost," Elsa says. "And you're kissing Miss Margie. Who are you?"

"Elsa, this is my friend Jon. Yes, he is a ghost and he's come to visit."

"I've come to stay, if that's okay. I don't want to go back to that lonely cemetery." He looks to Mom for confirmation. She nods and he beams.

Elsa seems put out. "But I stay with Miss Margie."

"There's room for all of us," I say.

Elsa glances around the house. "Is there? Maybe he can stay in Keaton's room." There's an ornery glint to her eye.

"That's not nice," Mom and I say at the same time.

"What's wrong with Keaton's room?" Holtzberry asks.

"That's a long story. Let's not get into it right now," I say. "Elsa, you're right. This place is full. Why don't you help me move some of these things into the garage while Mom and Jon say hello again?"

Elsa scrunches her face for a moment, then says, "Fine. But one question first. If he is Miss Margie's boyfriend, then how come he's a ghost? Why is he dead?"

Holtzberry rubs his full mustache and lets go of Mom. "You're old enough for the truth," he tells Elsa. "I was murdered. And I think by the same person that killed Margie."

I expect Elsa to be surprised, or scared, or something. "Oh," she says with a shrug. "I hoped it was something cool like a skydiving accident."

She picks up a stack of pans I bought at a garage sale and added to a pile here in the dining room never to be used. She carries the box to the garage door. "Can you open this for me, Rylan? It's hard to carry things and open doors at the same time."

I open the door for her, and she sits the pans on top of the stack in the garage. I put all my stuff from my apartment in the garage when I moved in here after Mom's death. I never opened most of the boxes, just left them piled up here. I suddenly feel overwhelmed by the whole mess. The house is full, the garage is full. Ford has tried to clear things out, but the trash bin only holds so much at a time.

"You need a dumpster," Holtzberry says, seeing my distress when I return to the kitchen.

"I need a lot of things," I say. The pain in my side has returned and I feel weak after being up and moving so much today. "Right now, I need a pain pill." I cross to the cabinet and find my bottle. It's almost empty. I hope the doctor will give me another refill.

"Maybe you should go lie down for a while," Mom says.

"We can keep moving stuff out while you rest," Elsa says. "Can you move boxes?" she asks Holtzberry. "I can."

He reaches for a box, but his hands go right through it. "I guess not."

"Too bad," Elsa says and picks up one that is way too big for her. She manages to get it to the garage, though. "See, I can. I can do lots of things."

"That's wonderful."

He's trying, but the gruff side of him is creeping back in. I get the feeling he isn't used to spending time with children. I wonder about his daughter, Brandie. Has he seen her since he passed? I tell myself this isn't the time to ask.

I stand in the kitchen after I take my pill and watch the three ghosts. My life sure has gotten strange in the last few years. Strange, but much fuller. It makes me happy.

Now if only I can solve Mom's murder. Is James Frazier really the killer? Holtzberry seems to think so.

I want to talk to Ford about it. He can access all the files and check if what Holtzberry said about Frazier being on the scene at all the deaths is true; that might mean something.

But checking all the files might have been what got Holtzberry killed...

There has to be another way.

SIXTEEN
ELSA WHITE

I move boxes and things to the garage all day, but the house still feels too full. I'm used to the stuff, I'm not used to all the people, alive and dead. Miss Margie and that Jon have been in her room all day talking and laughing. I should be happy for her, but I'm just annoyed. Why did he have to come to the house? When will he leave?

Rylan slept most of the day, so I couldn't talk with her. I hate that she got stabbed. Hate to see her hurting. I'm so glad she's getting better.

When Ford came back, he went into her room and hasn't come out. I can hear them talking through the door. I know Rylan said it was rude to listen at doors, but there's nothing else to do.

Sounds like they're talking about murder. It's always murder around here. It gets really old. Talk about something fun for a change.

With Miss Margie in her room with that Jon and Rylan and Ford in her room, there's nowhere for me to go. Nowhere to be.

I sit in the cleared dining room all alone, staring out the patio door as the sun sets.

I'm bored.

And lonely.

A house full of people and ghosts and I sit here alone.

As I have a lot lately, I think about my mom and dad. I miss them terribly. What's the point of still being here if I can't talk to the ones I love?

The dining room grows dark and still I sit. No one seems to notice where I am or what I'm doing. No one is thinking about me at all.

Mom would.

Dad would.

I close my eyes and focus on them.

When I open my eyes, I'm in my backyard. Through the lighted windows, I can see Mom in the kitchen. Dad is in the living room watching a basketball game. It's strange watching them from outside. I could go in—. I just have to wish myself there. That seems more sad to be in the room with them and they don't know it.

I wander over to the swing set I loved. I sit on the swing and, focusing hard, I make the swing move. It feels wonderful, almost like being alive. I swing and watch Mom through the kitchen window.

She looks up and stares out the window.

Can she sense me?

"Mom?" I whisper. "Come out and play."

"I'll play with you," a low voice says from dark. Roland sits on the swing next to me, his wooden toes just barely touching the weeds grown under the swing.

I stop swinging. "I'm not supposed to talk to you."

"Who says? Rylan?" He draws her name out, making it sound mean.

"She says you're dangerous."

"Do you think I'm dangerous? What have I done?"

He has me there. I don't know for sure he has done

anything. Rylan thinks he's behind a bunch of bad things that have happened in Ashby, but what if she's wrong?

I start swinging again. "Well, have you done awful things the way she says?"

"Depends on your point of view," he responds reasonably, kicking his thin legs to make the swing move.

"What do you want from me? I'm just a kid."

"Again, point of view is everything. To you, you're just a kid. Reality is very different."

I don't understand, but I don't argue. At least he's paying attention to me.

Through the window, Mom looks out again. She leans toward the glass and looks even closer. She says something to Dad, and he walks to the patio door leading onto the backyard.

"They saw me," Roland says. "Goodbye, Elsa." He jumps from the swing and runs across the yard into the shadows.

Dad opens the patio door. "Who's out there?" he calls. Mom stands behind him, looking directly at me.

I kick harder to make the swing move faster. Will they notice?

"I saw something right there on the swing. It was small like a child," Mom says.

"I don't see anything now." Dad turns to go back into the house, but Mom stops him.

"The swing." She points at me. "It's moving."

"Probably the wind," Dad says.

"There isn't any wind."

I kick harder, making the swing really fly. "I'm here!" I shout. "I'm here!"

Mom steps from the patio toward the swing set. "Do you think it's her?" she asks, breathless.

"It's not Elsa. No matter what that crazy lady told you, Elsa is not a ghost." He sounds like he's trying to convince himself.

"But I'm here, Dad. I'm right here."

"You're probably right," Mom says, her eyes lingering on where I am. "I just miss her so much."

"I know, but believing she's a ghost is not the way to deal with that. We just have to accept that she's never coming home to us." Dad puts his hands on Mom's shoulders and leads her back to the house.

"Come back!" I shout.

He looks over his shoulder, and, just for a moment, I think he might have heard me. "I wish she was," he whispers before closing the door.

I stop swinging. There's no point to it. No joy in it anymore.

SEVENTEEN
ROLAND THE MARIONETTE

Visiting Elsa was a risk I shouldn't have taken. I have been careful so far. I've wreaked all the havoc I wanted without getting caught.

Tonight, I was seen by her mom. That is unacceptable.

But I want her.

I need her.

She's like the daughter Jean could never give me.

Thinking of Jean makes me boil.

That woman deserved to be thrown from the balcony at the courthouse. Good riddance.

Of course, that act is what got me stuck in this puppet. I don't regret it, though. I had a good life. I got away with everything and died without anyone knowing the monster I truly am.

Monster. I like that word.

I have to hide that side of myself from Elsa, though.

The future depends on it.

Her presence made me stronger. Her hands released me from that prison Rylan locked me in.

I owe everything to Elsa.

And nothing to Rylan.

"Ryyyylaaann," I cry out into the night, not caring who can hear me.

She's the beginning and the end of my troubles. She's the one in the way.

It's time to return to the farm where this all started. Time to remind him of what he truly is and what must be done.

I rub my hands together in excitement, the strings above my head swaying.

EIGHTEEN
RYLAN FLYNN

"Rylan, Brett just called and told me you have something you need to tell everyone," Aunt Val immediately says when I answer the phone in the morning.

Dad has a big mouth, is what I want to say. It was hard enough telling him about Mom, but I should have known he wouldn't be able to resist telling his sister. I should have prepared for this. It's a big secret, but there was no way I could keep it forever.

"Good morning, Aunt Val," I say, keeping my voice low so as not to disturb Ford who slept through the ringtone. I creep out of bed and sneak into the hall. The rest of the house is still quiet. "What time is it?" I ask with a yawn.

"The sun is up?"

"Not everyone is up with the sun," I point out. Since she opens her donut shop first thing every morning, Val is a very early riser.

"This couldn't wait. What is this about? He said it was important and about your mom. Did they figure out who killed her?"

I wish I could say yes. "It's not that," I say as I fish out my bottle of pain pills from the cabinet.

"Stop being vague. It must be big because he wants to hold a family meeting at the cabin this morning. I've already called Keaton. He was up."

Was that a dig?

Val doesn't do that.

I check the time. It's only just now seven.

The thought of facing my brother with the news that his mom's ghost has been here for years without him knowing makes my stomach hurt more than it already does.

"I will be there within the hour. Does that work?"

"Good. I'll make pancakes." Val loves feeding people. She can't help herself.

I say goodbye and take the pain pill. Standing in the kitchen, the house feels at peace. No one is up yet. Not even Elsa who rarely rests.

Come to think of it, the house has been too quiet. Did I even see Elsa last night?

I don't remember seeing her. Ford and I were so busy talking about the cases all evening. We even checked in with Mom and Holtzberry to discuss all the angles.

That was an interesting meeting, with me repeating everything they said to Ford. It kind of made my head hurt but was also kind of fun. I'm used to figuring things out on my own. It's nice to have a team to bounce ideas off. Not that it helped. We didn't get any closer to a suspect in Mom's murder. James Frazier seems the most likely one, but I still have a hard time believing that.

But did we see Elsa in all that time?

I don't think so.

I head down the hall to Mom's door, but it's closed and I don't want to open it if Holtzberry is in there with her. I'm sure he is. He vowed not to leave her side now that they've been reunited.

But if they're both in the room together, where is Elsa?

There's only one other room that is remotely useable.

Keaton's room.

I don't want to open that door, so stand in the hall with my hand on the knob. Would Elsa go in here after what happened with Roland?

I need to check. I turn the knob and push the door open slowly. "Elsa? Are you in here?"

She's lying on the bed, staring at the ceiling. The room is covered with crosses on all walls and even on the window. The pale morning light barely breaks the dim.

"About time someone noticed I was gone," Elsa says.

I sit on the bed next to her. "How long have you been in here?"

"Since last night. When I got back, you were all in Miss Margie's room talking about those dumb murders. I didn't know where else to go."

"I'm so sorry. We are all caught up in the cases, I know. But you shouldn't be in here. It's dangerous."

"You say everything is dangerous. Roland is nice, by the way. Not at all like you say."

This shocks me. And did she say 'got back'? "Where did you go last night?"

She turns on her side and faces the wall. "I went to see my parents. I stayed outside on the swings." She sounds heartbroken.

"What happened?"

"Roland came and swung with me for a while. Then Mom saw him, and he ran off." She rolls over to face me. "Why can't I have a friend? You have Ford, and Miss Margie has that Jon. I don't have anyone."

I hate to see the pain in her tiny face. Am I being selfish keeping her here? Should I try to cross her to Heaven? In my heart, I feel Elsa is still here for a reason beyond the fact that I want her with us.

"I don't know the answer to that," I tell her. "I do understand feeling lonely, though."

"I'm not lonely. I'm bored." I don't believe her words, but I go along with it.

"I know there isn't much to do here for a little girl, let alone a ghost. Tell you what, do you want to go to Aunt Val's with me? She has a lovely black lab that you can visit with even if he doesn't know you're there."

Elsa sits up. "I haven't been to your aunt's house yet." Her mood changes instantly like only a child's can. "What's his name?"

"It's George. He's the best dog. You'll like him. Now, let's get out of this room."

I reach for her hand, but mine goes through hers and grows cold. Sometimes, I still forget Elsa isn't alive.

I wake Ford up to tell him I'm going to the family meeting. I would invite him to come too, but he has to work. There is a lot to look into. Holtzberry's suspicions about Frazier, Mom's suspicions about Charlie Landry's death not being an accident, and Ford's own suspicions about Jacob McClure's car accident. So many suspicions and I'm going to a family meeting just about Mom's ghost.

How I wish Dad had kept the news to himself. I have enough going on without having my whole family mad at me for keeping such an important secret.

Soon, Ford is off to work, and my Cadillac is full of ghosts as we drive to Val's. Mom wanted to be there, and she wouldn't leave Holtzberry behind. They sit in the back seat together, holding hands. I'm happy for them, but it's a little too much. Although I can't blame them. They thought they'd only meet again in heaven. This must be a wonderful treat. Plus, Mom must be overjoyed that he didn't shoot her. I can't even imagine believing that about Ford. It would break my heart.

Elsa sits in the front seat. She grows excited when we pull in and George runs out to greet us. "He's so cute," she squeals. "You should get a dog. Onyx is fine, but a dog would be better."

"I think we have enough going on at home. We don't need a dog too," I mutter, parking the car.

When I check the rearview, I notice Mom's face looks stricken.

"You'll be fine," Holtzberry reassures her. "Remember, they all love you."

"That's what I'm afraid of. I haven't seen Val in a long time. She and I were very close, even after I divorced her brother. It will be nice to see her again, but I'm still nervous."

Keaton's BMW pulls in next to us. Mom stares, rapt, as my brother climbs out of the car. "Keaton," she whispers. "My boy."

"Let's get this over with," I say, a bit annoyed and hating myself for it. I climb out of the car and pet George as I wait for Keaton to catch up. "You didn't bring Cheryl?" I try to act surprised but am secretly relieved his fiancée isn't here. Unlike Mom and Val, we may be almost sisters-in-law, but we are not close. In fact, I get the feeling she actively dislikes me but hides it for Keaton's sake.

"She has to work," Keaton says, his voice clipped. "I should be at work too, but both Dad and Val asked me to come. So here I am. Another crazy puppet on the loose?"

I glance at Mom who stands close to Keaton, although he can't tell that, of course. "No," I say. "We'll get to it in a minute. I think Val made pancakes." I turn and head up to the porch of my aunt's A-frame cabin.

"Nice place," Holtzberry says and nods at my mom. "I came and talked to Valerie about your case back then, but it was dark." He admires the trees surrounding the cabin. "I didn't realize the woods here were so thick," he says, almost to himself.

Elsa is trying to pet George. He barks in response, clearly sensing something nearby. "He feels me," Elsa exclaims.

Mom is behind Keaton who is already complaining about how long this is taking. She's murmuring about how handsome he is and how she's so happy to see him.

Aunt Val comes out on the porch and greets us. With everything going on, both in the real world and the ghost realm, I'm starting to get overwhelmed.

George barks again and Elsa shouts, "I did that!"

"Elsa, stop scaring the dog," I say sharply.

Everyone immediately stops talking and the birdsong is now the only sound on the porch.

"Rylan?" Val asks. "Who's Elsa?"

"Can we just eat first and then I'll explain everything?"

"Of course," Val says with her usual good nature. "Brett is pulling in now." She looks to the lane. "Let's eat."

We all go into the small open-concept cabin, everyone's mood subdued. Val's boyfriend, Sawyer, is behind the stove in the kitchen, flipping pancakes.

Great, another person I have to confess to.

I instantly regret my pessimistic thought. I like Sawyer, and he and Val are so close now, he might as well be family. I guess it makes sense to tell everyone about Mom at the same time.

Keaton sits at the dining table with Mom hovering close by. "Smells good," he says about the pancakes.

The tension I caused on the porch dissipates. Holtzberry is looking around the cabin as if he's searching for something and Elsa is still trying to play with George, but the dog is now ignoring her, his chin on his paws.

Dad walks in and catches my eye. "Is she here?" he mouths.

I nod as I sit myself down at the table.

Dad looks around as if he will be able to see Mom. I motion

with my head to the seat beside Keaton, and Dad stares hard at the air there.

"Pancakes are ready," Val says, setting a platter of steaming cakes on the table.

All the living people sit, and Dad says a prayer. He adds, "and thank you for the news Rylan is going to share," before his amen, which focuses everyone's attention on me.

I want to run. I don't want to tell them about Mom.

I feel my family's eyes on me. Even George is staring at me.

"It's okay, Ry. You can do this," Mom says from her seat next to Keaton.

"Go ahead," Dad prompts gently.

"You all know I can see ghosts." I don't know where to start, so I begin with the obvious.

Val senses my distress. "Of course, dear. Is this about ghosts?"

"Yes. Anyway..." I clear my throat.

"Get to the point already," Elsa says. "They aren't going to bite you."

I look around the table, my mouth dry and my stomach flipping. "There are ghosts here with us right now. Elsa, a little girl that was stuck inside a stuffed bear, is sitting beside George." They all look toward the dog. Elsa waves although they can't see her.

"Over there by the door is Detective Jon Holtzberry, who you might remember as the detective from Mom's murder case."

Holtzberry rubs his ample mustache and nods to the table.

I keep going before I lose my nerve. "And next to you, Keaton, in that empty chair, is Mom."

I expected an uproar, or at least some reaction, but Keaton doesn't even look at the chair. "That's not funny," he says to me, his voice heavy with anger.

"I'm not trying to be funny. She's really here. She's been at the house since just after the funeral." I look down at my plate and the untouched pancake sticky with syrup.

"Mom is here? Like her ghost is here?" Keaton asks, incredulous.

"That's what this meeting is for," Dad says. "Rylan told me yesterday."

Keaton jumps from his chair and steps away from the table.

"Keaton, don't be scared. I'm here." Mom reaches out to him, as if she'll be able to touch him.

"She says, 'don't be scared'," I repeat.

"I'm not scared," he says. "I'm angry." He turns away from her chair and stares at me. "You've known since the funeral?" His voice rises. "And you didn't tell anyone? You kept me from my dead mother? The girl, the detective, I don't even know what to say about them, but Mom? How could you?"

I've never seen my brother so mad at me. But I know I deserve it.

"I don't know why I didn't tell you. I didn't tell anyone. I just—"

"Don't give me that crap. You kept her to yourself because you wanted to hurt me. To hurt all of us."

"Now, Keaton," Dad and Mom say at the same time.

"Don't come to her defense like you always do." He turns his wrath on Dad now. "She needs to be held accountable for her actions. She hid the puppet thing from us and now this."

"'This' is your mother," Dad admonishes him.

Keaton freezes, suddenly realizing the implications. "If you're really here, I'm sorry I'm getting so upset. But how do we know this isn't some crazy plot by her? She could be doing this for attention."

That stings. It really stings.

Mom stands up from her chair and gets in front of Keaton's reddening face. "I'm here. I've always been here," she says, reaching to touch his hair. "Tell him to remember his dreams from last night. It wasn't a dream, I was in his room." Keaton's hair moves and he flinches.

"She says to remember your dreams from last night. She says she was actually in your room. It wasn't a dream."

Keaton's knees buckle a bit, and he has to sit down. "I did dream about her last night. I dream about her often. Every time, she's watching over me." Mom touches his hair again and he puts his hand up to touch it too. "Is that her making my hair move?"

"It is," I say gently. It's like we all are holding our breath, waiting for his reaction.

"Mom?" he says, his voice barely a whisper.

I hear Val sniffle and see tears in her eyes. "Margie's really here," she says. "We missed you."

Mom turns to face everyone else. "I missed you all. Well, I don't know this one, but I'm sure I would have missed him too," she says of Sawyer. This makes me laugh in relief.

I tell them what she said, and they all laugh nervously.

"Why now?" Keaton asks. "Does this have to do with the escaped puppet?"

I look for Holtzberry's reaction. He's staring hard at me. We told him about the puppet last night and how I thought it might be connected to the many deaths in Ashby. He wasn't sold on the idea. He barely believed Roland existed.

"I think the puppet is tied to the recent murders, but I'm not sure if he's tied to Mom's. Most likely whatever evil is in him is also in whoever shot her, though." Keaton flinches at the word 'shot' and I make a mental note to be more gentle with my words in future. "As to why I'm telling you this now, that's because she asked me to help solve her case."

"That makes sense," Val says reasonably.

"Is that why the ghost of the detective is here too?" Keaton asks.

"Partly that. Partly because they were dating when Mom died and he wanted to see her again."

Keaton takes this new revelation better than the first. "She was dating the detective? He never said anything about that at the time."

"He had his reasons," I say. "He only wanted what was best for her case. Who would try harder to find her killer than the man who loved her?"

"Still. That's a conflict of interest," Keaton pushes.

"Well, he's passed away now, so it's a moot point."

"How did he die?" Sawyer joins the conversation.

"Officially, it was listed as a heart attack, but he says he was murdered for looking into the suspicious deaths in Ashby, including Mom's."

"So many deaths," Val muses. "How is that possible?"

"He thinks there's a serial killer in town." I drop the words and the room grows quiet.

NINETEEN
MARGIE FLYNN

It hurts sitting in a room with my loved ones and not actually being with them. I've gotten so used to living with Rylan, I sometimes forget I'm not actually alive.

After Rylan drops the bombshell comment about a serial killer possibly terrorizing Ashby, there's a moment of silence, then a flurry of words. Everyone talks at once, over each other, asking questions she doesn't have answers to.

Jon tries to fill in where he can, telling her the answers. We discussed all this last night, and I don't want to hear it again. The thought that a deranged killer broke into my house and shot me in my sleep makes my blood boil. All of this almost makes me miss the long stretch of time I blocked the knowledge, survived in a fog. I wasn't ready to face the fact that I'm actually dead.

It still hurts.

I stop listening to the discussion about killers and murders and look for Elsa. This can't be good for her to listen to. I expect to see her playing with George, but she's not there.

"Where's Elsa?" I ask Rylan and Jon, but they're so involved in the killer conversation, they don't hear me. I stand up and go out on the porch to search for her. The porch is empty as is the tiny yard between the cabin and the woods.

Where else would she go?

"Elsa!" I call. "Where are you?"

Twitters and birdsong come from the woods, but no little girl.

I'm sure she's fine. Just sure of it. Besides, what can happen to her?

But something niggles at my motherly intuition. What if the puppet has her? Panic immediately seizes my guts, and I begin wringing my hands. Would he hurt her?

The door opens behind me, and Rylan steps out onto the porch. "You okay out here?"

"Not really. Elsa is missing. I can't find her."

Rylan scans the woods and the parking area. "I think I see her." She points to the Cadillac.

Sure enough, I can see Elsa in the back seat. "Guess she got tired of the murder talk."

"I'm sorry. I know this can't be easy on you."

"It's important work. Just find out who did this to me."

"We will," she says resolutely before turning and going back inside.

I focus hard and soon find myself in the back seat next to Elsa. She doesn't even seem to notice me when I appear, just keeps staring out the window at Keaton's silver BMW sedan.

"What you doing?" I ask.

She shrugs one shoulder but doesn't look at me.

"Did you get bored? That talk was kind of hard to listen to."

"I guess," she says. "All of you keep talking and talking about the same things. Why doesn't Rylan just go get the bad guy like she usually does?" She slumps further into the seat and crosses her arms.

"She doesn't know who it is yet. That's why they are discussing it."

"She isn't going to catch him by talking about it."

Elsa has a good point. We need to take action to catch this guy before he kills someone else. I suddenly have an idea.

"Will you be okay if Jon and I go somewhere?"

"Why would I care?" She's trying to sound disinterested, but I hear the waver in her voice.

"I don't like leaving you alone."

"Then take me with you."

"Because a police station is not a place for a little girl."

"We went there on a field trip once. It was boring. I don't want to go anyway." She wraps her arms tighter around herself.

"We won't be gone long. When I get back, we can read some more books."

This perks her up. "Promise?"

"I do. Now be a good girl and come sit on the porch where Rylan can see you."

She follows me to the porch and takes a seat on one of the rockers. I notice she makes the chair swing back and forth. She's getting really powerful. I can barely move anything even when I focus hard.

I find Jon inside and tell him I want to go to the police station to see this James Frazier for myself. If he's our prime suspect in my murder and the other murders, I should at least know what he looks like.

The conversation has moved on from suspects, and I can tell it's wrapping up. We let Rylan know we're leaving, and I take another long look at Keaton. He may be all grown up now, but he's still my baby boy and my first born.

"Let's go," Jon says, taking my hand. We focus hard on the station and when I open my eyes, we are at the front doors.

"Where would Frazier be?" I ask.

"If he's here, he's probably in the bull pen. We'll start there."

I feel nervous as Jon leads me through the station. Do I really want to come face to face with my killer? What reason would he have to kill me? The working theory is because I suspected Charlie Landry didn't die in a hunting accident, and Frazier might have had something to do with that too.

Was that a reason to kill me? I'd already told Jon, the only person that it would have mattered to anyway.

That brings me back to Jon as the killer. I look at the man beside me, helping me. He couldn't have done it. He loves me. My heart tells me so.

But hearts can be wrong.

I feel so confused and mixed up I barely know which way we are walking.

"That's Frazier over there." Jon points across a room full of tiny desks and blue uniforms. A dark-haired young man talks to another, older, man.

I lock eyes on Frazier, certain I'll feel a ripple of recognition if he was the one who shot me. I walk across the room to get a better look, but he's a complete stranger to me.

"Who's he talking to?" I turn back to Jon.

"That's Chief McKay."

I walk close to Frazier, look him up and down. "Doesn't look like a serial killer," I say.

"They never do. That's how they get away with it."

"You know he's given Rylan a lot of grief since she started helping with cases. He's not very nice to her."

"Just adds to the pile of evidence against him."

Frazier's words to the chief seem respectful, but his body language says he's getting frustrated. I focus my attention on what they're saying.

"Come with me," McKay says and leads Frazier away down a hall. Jon and I follow.

As we get further up the hall, I notice somebody I recognize walking toward us. Ford. McKay stops him too and asks him to come to his office.

Once we are all in the office, McKay sits at his desk. Ford and Frazier flank the door, both of them looking tense.

"I always hated it when McKay called me in here," Jon mutters. "This can't be good."

"I have a problem with both of you, and I wonder if it's connected," McKay starts. "You both know I can see what cases you look into on the computer, right?"

Ford and Frazier say "yes" at the same time.

"Then, Pierce, tell me why you are looking into all the homicides that Frazier was on the scene at?"

Ford's shoulders tighten. "I'm just working an angle."

"An angle about me?" Frazier asks, clearly angry.

"Not just you. I'm looking into something."

"You should be looking into the break-ins and vandalism like I told you. Closed cases are closed. Especially ones that are accidents or natural deaths," McKay says. "Now, what is your interest in searching Frazier?"

I feel bad for Ford. He can't exactly say a ghost told him to look into it.

"I'm not looking into him particularly. He just shows up in the files," he tries.

McKay's face grows stern. "You searched his name."

Ford shuffles his feet. "Okay, so I did. It has come to my attention that he was on the scene at a bunch of suspicious deaths. I was just seeing if that was true."

"Who told you that?" Frazier demands.

"I found a note from Detective Holtzberry." A good answer.

"Holtzberry is dead," Frazier says.

"That's one of the cases I'm looking into. He died in his sleep of a heart attack. Seems pretty convenient that you were the one first on the scene." He looks at Frazier with challenge in his eyes.

Frazier balls his fists. "What are you insinuating?"

"I'm not insinuating anything. Like I said, I'm working a hunch."

McKay has been listening and now cuts in. "Pierce, a bunch of coincidences don't add up to suspicion."

"It does when it leads to murder."

"How dare you!" Frazier shouts, the fists still balled and now barely held in check.

"And what about Margie Flynn?" Ford pushes. "Her death was an obvious murder and you were the first on the scene at that one too. You telling us you were on patrol at all the cases?"

I move right behind Ford's shoulder and lean in close to hear the answer to this question.

"I didn't hurt her either," Frazier says. "Maybe you should look into that girlfriend of yours. She's the one that found the body and she's the one that inherited everything. Sounds like a perfect motive for murder."

I can't believe the turn this conversation just took. My blood boils and I ball my own fists. I want to hit the man accusing my daughter of my murder. I want to hurt him the way he hurt us all.

In a flash, I'm sure Jon is right. This man is the killer.

I lose control of my anger and flail my fists at Frazier's face. I pass right through him, and he barely notices. I focus harder and swing again. This time, I connect with his jaw, and he flinches in pain and shock.

"Did you just hit me?" he asks Ford.

"I would like to, but I didn't even move."

"Now men, let's calm down here," McKay says. "No one hit anyone else, and no one is accusing the other of murder. Let's be civil."

Jon tries to calm me, too, putting his hand on my shoulder. I shake it off and walk across the room, facing away from the men.

"We obviously have a problem here," McKay says.

I stare at the shelves in front of me, not really seeing the objects on display, trying not to cry. Maybe facing my killer wasn't a good idea.

A framed photo catches my eye. It's of McKay and two other men in hunting clothes in front of a dead deer. I focus on the man on the right.

"Jon, come look at this."

He joins me and looks to where I point.

"That's Charlie Landry. And he's hunting with McKay."

We both turn to look at the chief.

"Could he be the killer?" I whisper.

TWENTY

TERESA GRANT

I only need the last piece of the puzzle on the table and I'm done. The serene beach scene only took me three days even though it is a thousand pieces. Well, nine hundred ninety-nine. There's a small gap in a palm tree that is missing. The blank place bothers me. It feels undone and makes me itchy inside.

The piece isn't on the table, so I search the floor for it. There is a tatty cat toy under the table, but no puzzle piece.

"Lucky, did you take it?" I ask the room in general, speaking to my gray tabby. He's notorious for stealing small things and hiding them.

Lucky sits at the window, blinking at me with cat disinterest.

If he has the piece, I'll never get it back.

I run my hand over the finished work, enjoying the light rippled feeling of the surface. I love puzzles. They give me something to fill in the empty hours.

So many empty hours.

You'd think after eight years of being a widow, I'd get used to the quiet house. The radio constantly plays a talk radio station, an attempt to fill the void my husband left. The voices are better than the silence, but it's still too quiet.

My soul isn't, though. I'm on edge.

I always get like this when I finish a puzzle. As long as I have something to focus on, I do okay. Otherwise, my mind gets away from me. Sometimes, I distract myself with replaying conversations with Gene. I try to pull one up in my memory now, but all I see is his face in the coffin with so much makeup and embalming I barely recognized him.

I shake my head to clear it. I don't want to think of Gene like that. I want to remember his smile, his laugh, the way he used to hold me at night.

I wish I had a session with Pastor Flynn today. The times in his office feel like the only times I'm truly alive; the only times someone is listening, the only times someone seems to care.

Even Lucky barely cares. I call his name, and he doesn't bother to look my way.

I can't sit still, so I jump up from my chair. Well, what passes for jumping at this point in my life. At eighty-six, my jumping days are long behind me. Once on my feet, I go to the kitchen window and indulge in my guilty pleasure of looking through the binoculars I keep on the sill.

I like to say I'm birdwatching. Sometimes, I am. Just enough to make it legit. There's no one here to answer to anyway. If I happen to see what the neighbors are doing while looking at birds, who's to stop me?

Out here in the country, there aren't many neighbors to watch. From this window, I can see the farm across the street. Not much happens there. He lives alone and works a lot. I scan his front yard and the nearest barn, but I don't see any movement.

I hadn't expected any.

I turn the binoculars on my favorite house. It's down the road and barely visible across the field separating their place from mine. This house has four kids living there, and they are often out in the backyard running or digging or just being kids.

I like watching them. It reminds me of the years I taught Sunday School. Gene was still alive then and life was golden. That feels like another life entirely.

No matter how hard I search, I don't see any movement at that house either. Slow day around here. I have one last house I can see from here, but I have to go on the front porch to see it properly. I'm so bored, I decide to check it out.

There's a slight nip in the late spring air when I step outside, and I find myself wishing I had grabbed a jacket. I'll just see if there is anything worth watching before I decide to stay out here any longer. As I turn to look at the house to the west, I see movement across the street.

Excited way more than I should be, I lift the binoculars and focus on the front yard. A small child is walking across the yard. At first, I think it's one of the kids from next door, but when I look closer, I realize it's not a child.

At least not one like I've ever seen before.

I drop the binoculars in shock. Is that a marionette walking across the yard?

Putting the lenses back to my eyes, I adjust the focus. As difficult as it is for me to believe, there is indeed a stringed jester puppet scurrying across the grass. The front door opens and the man that lives across the road lets the puppet inside.

He must sense me watching because he looks directly at me. Busted.

I drop the binoculars, but it's too late. He caught me spying. And, judging by his expression, he is none too happy I saw him with that thing.

What *was* that thing?

With shaking hands, I lift the binoculars to my eyes once more. The puppet has come back to the doorway and is staring at me too, his large red mouth hanging open.

The man gives one last glare my way, then they both go inside, and he shuts the door.

I put a hand to my chest, my heart pounding.

What did I just see?

I lie in bed, staring into the darkness, my mind swirling between missing Gene, like I do every night, and wondering about the neighbor and his puppet that walks on his own.

Am I losing my mind? At my age, the mind can begin to slip. Have I crossed a line and lost it?

A weight lands on my bed, and I flinch, crying out softly. A loud and angry meow tells me it's just Lucky.

Did I feed him tonight?

I can't remember. After what I saw at the neighbor's, I don't remember much. The day passed in a blur. I recall putting the TV on at one point, but I can't remember what I watched. I even forgot about finding the missing puzzle piece.

Lucky meows again, so I throw off the covers. I'm not sleeping anyway, I might as well check that he's been fed.

On bare feet, I go downstairs to the kitchen cupboard where I keep Lucky's food. As I'm pulling out the bag, the floor squeaks behind me.

I spin around, and there he is, the man from across the street, standing before me with a rope in his hands. We've never met, but I recognize him immediately from all the times I've watched him.

"You should have learned to mind your own business," he snarls.

I drop the bag of cat food, and it spills across the floor. I'm frozen in fear. Why does he have a rope?

"I'm sorry," I stammer. "I shouldn't have been snooping."

Behind his leg, I see the thing I saw earlier in the yard, the live jester marionette. It steps out and laughs. The puppet scares me more than the man.

I turn to run, but there is nowhere to go in the small kitchen. They block the only exit. Like a cornered animal, I dart back and forth, looking for an opening.

The man grabs me by the hair and shoves me to my knees with a grunt. The puppet jumps on my back, and I feel the strings wrap around my neck.

I claw at the strings, scratching myself in the process. They tighten until I can't breathe.

Shaking my head, I try to throw the horrible thing off my back. It clings to the strings, cackling.

"We need to do this right," the man says. "Here, let me do it." He sounds so excited it terrifies me.

I need air desperately, but the strings are too tight.

They're going to kill me.

I'm actually going to die.

The strings release, and for a moment, I think I'm saved. "Please," I beg, rubbing where the strings were and gasping.

"Too late," the man says and wraps the rope around my neck. He pulls me back and drags me into the living room. "Too bad you're so sad without your husband, you had to hang yourself," he says. To my horror, he wraps the rope around the banister and pulls hard.

My feet slide across the floor as I'm dragged up by the rope. I try to hold myself down, but soon even my toes don't touch the ground.

The rope tightens painfully, cutting off my air.

No, not now. Not like this.

I kick my feet into the empty air. I pull on the rope above my head, but I don't have the strength to relieve the weight on my neck.

The man watches as I struggle, a rapt expression on his face.

He is enjoying this. The puppet dances around him, kicking his tiny feet.

This has to be a nightmare. Maybe I'll wake up soon...

But no matter how I kick and squirm, I can't breathe. I'm not waking up.

My vision begins to dim, and my kicking slows.

The last thing I see is the missing puzzle piece on the floor.

My last project completed.

TWENTY-ONE
RYLAN FLYNN

"Rylan, come find me," she calls in my dream. "You need to find me."

I fight the dream, struggle to gain consciousness. "Where are you?" I ask.

She hangs from the end of a rope tied to a banister.

The shock of the image wakes me, and I sit up in bed.

I blink several times until my room comes into focus. My leather jacket is thrown on the chair. My clothes are on the floor.

Ford is in my bed.

The fear from the dream subsides when I see his naked chest, rising and falling, next to me. I lay back down next to him, but the voice from my dream won't leave my mind.

My Sunday School teacher needs me.

I press against Ford, not wanting to face the truth.

Wherever she is, she's dead and her spirit is calling to me.

I have to help her however I can.

I wriggle to the end of the bed and climb out, trying not to disturb Ford. He wakes anyway.

"What time is it?" he asks.

I check my phone. "Just after six."

"Why are you up already?" he groans.

"I have to check on someone."

This grabs his attention, and he hauls himself up on one elbow, rubbing his eyes. "On whom?"

"Remember when I told you I ran into my Sunday School teacher, Teresa Grant? Well... I think she is dead and her spirit is calling to me."

"Why do you think she's dead?" He climbs out of bed and begins to dress.

"I just saw her in a dream. She was hanging from some stairs. She said, 'come find me'."

"You don't usually dream of spirits. You sure this is something?" He pulls on his shirt. Despite the serious situation, I find myself sorry to see his bare chest disappear.

"I'm not sure of anything. I just want to be sure." I have one shoe on and am searching for my other Chuck Taylor. I find it under the bed.

"What are you going to do?"

"I'll get her address from Dad and then go to her house. If she's dead like I think she is, I'll call it in."

"I don't like this," he says, taking me by the shoulders.

"I don't either, but here we are. If she isn't a spirit, I wouldn't be able to hear her. If it's just a dream, I'll find her safe and sound."

"I hope it's safe and sound." He hesitates. "Why don't you wait until after I get off work, then we can both go?"

I shake my head. "No. I'll go now. I just hope Dad's awake to give me her address."

I kiss him goodbye and sneak out of the house before Mom or Holtzberry or even Elsa realizes I'm leaving.

Dad answers on the third ring. "Hey, Dad. I need your help," I say as I climb into my car.

He sounds sleepy. "What can I do?"

"I need an address for Teresa Grant. I imagine you have it in your office computer."

"I have my computer here at the house. I can look it up."

I love that he goes along with my strange requests, doesn't ask too many questions. "Great, I'm on my way."

I pull out onto the quiet street and zoom through town to Dad's.

The front porch light is on as always, and I warm at the familiar welcoming sight. I hurry down the walk and let myself into the house.

"I'm in the kitchen," Dad calls when he hears me. I find him in sweatpants and a T-shirt, a stark difference from the button-up shirt and slacks he normally wears. His hair sticks up in the back. I like this side of him. I see him often, but it's always for the show or for a case. When's the last time I came here and just hung out with my dad? I realize it's been an embarrassingly long time. I make a mental note to change that as soon as things slow down.

Dad hands me a slip of paper with an address written on it. "You going to tell me what this is about or are you just going to run off?"

"I need to go. I think something happened to Teresa. I saw her in a dream. Her spirit sort of called out to me."

"Her spirit? Wait! You think she's dead?"

"I do. I saw her hanging from her stairs."

Dad rubs the sticking-up hair. "I have been afraid of a thing like that happening. Teresa is a lonely woman. Suicide is more common than you'd think in senior citizens."

"Suicide is one possibility."

"You have another?"

I cock my head and twist my lips in answer.

"You're thinking murder?"

"I won't know until I see her, but there's a reason she called to me."

"Why don't you call the police or, better yet, have Ford do a welfare check on her?"

"Ford doesn't do welfare checks and he's busy with the other cases. Besides, how would he explain it? Tell everyone I had a dream?"

"Good point." He walks to the hall. "Wait a minute and I'll come with you." I open my mouth to argue, but he holds up his hand to stop me. "If she was hurt on purpose, there's no way I'm letting you go alone. It could be dangerous."

As Dad goes to change, I think about what Mickey said about it being dangerous to be around me. Maybe she was right and it's better she stays away.

I do miss her, though.

While I wait, I send her a quick text. "Thinking of you. Hope you're feeling okay." I add a heart emoji and hit send.

To my surprise, she texts right back. Just another heart emoji, but it's something and will have to do for now. I make another mental promise to spend more time with Mickey after this case as well—if she wants me to, I remind myself of how she doesn't want to see me. Seems like I haven't had any social interactions that don't revolve around cases or ghosts lately.

I need to change that.

But first I need to find Teresa Grant.

The address Dad gave me is down a rural road south of town. We pass some impressive farms. The one across the road from Teresa has several red barns and a set of tall silos. Even in my distracted state, I can't help admire the set-up.

Teresa's place is a pale comparison. Her home is just a smallish farmhouse from over a century ago with a single outbuilding that is in disrepair. The yard is tall and overgrown, even for spring. Weeds choke the flower beds flanking the porch.

"Her late husband, Gene, used to keep the place up," Dad says, clearly realizing what I'm thinking. "Teresa did her best for a while, but she gave in."

"You don't have to explain." I park on the weedy gravel drive, and we climb out.

The morning sun glows through the tall trees that are no doubt even older than the house. A few birds sing, but the property otherwise seems quiet. Even solemn.

"Do you think the door is locked?" I ask just above a whisper as we walk across the tall grass.

"Probably not."

The porch steps sag when we walk on them and the floorboards creak. Hoping we don't fall through, I cross to the wood and glass door. I try to look inside, but there's a curtain obscuring the view.

Dad looks through another window, cupping his hands.

"Can you see the stairs?" I ask.

"It's dark. I can't make anything out."

The doorknob looks original to the house and is rusted. I grip it tight, take a deep breath and turn. The door creaks open.

The inside of the house is dim despite the morning sun. My nerves are tight as I call, "Teresa, are you here?"

A gray blur darts across the hall leading to the rest of the house. I grab my chest and let out a nervous laugh.

"It's just her cat. His name is Lucky. She talks about him all the time," Dad says, stepping past me into the house.

"Teresa, it's Pastor Flynn and Rylan. Are you home?" He strides down the hall, but he stops short when he reaches the end. He raises a hand to his mouth. "Oh no."

I peer around the corner and my dream vision hangs before me.

Teresa Grant dangles at the end of a rope tied to the banister. Her feet are just six inches from the floor. Six inches too far.

"Poor Teresa," Dad whispers, reaching out to smooth her hair. "Why didn't you tell me? I could have helped you."

"I really don't think she did this to herself," I say, stepping closer to the body. "See these scratches on her throat? She was trying to get out of the rope."

"Maybe she changed her mind. Most people do before the end."

"Look here." I point to a set of thin lines just above the rope. "I had similar marks on my neck not long ago, just not as deep."

"What are they?"

"They're from strings pulled around the throat."

Dad takes a step back. "You mean puppet strings, don't you?"

"That's what it looks like to me."

"But the puppet couldn't tie her like this. She's too heavy for him."

The sober truth I realize I've been aware of all along hits me. "Someone is under his influence, and he did this."

TWENTY-TWO
RYLAN FLYNN

The silence is broken when the cat rushes back into the room and up the stairs.

"Poor Lucky," Dad says. "I'll have to find him a new home."

"Did Teresa have any other family?"

"Gene died several years ago. They never had kids. I think she has a sister that lives in Florida."

There's another long moment of silence as we reflect on the tragedy of the situation. Finally, I speak. "I suppose I should call this in. I'm not sure what I'm going to say. How do I explain why we came here? Ford and probably Tyler will believe in the dream thing I had, but what will they say in their report?"

"We could say Teresa had an appointment with me this morning but didn't show up, so I got worried."

"That doesn't explain why I'm here, though. Plus, it's super early for a missed appointment."

"Just call it in and let the chips fall where they will," Dad says. "I hate leaving her up on that rope. The sooner the coroner can come and get her down the better. I'd take her down myself, but if you're right and this is murder, I don't want to mess with the scene."

"On that note, let's go out so we can't be accused of interfering." With my phone to my ear, I lead us back out to the driveaway.

The phone rings so long, I'm afraid Ford won't answer, but he does eventually, sounding slightly out of breath. "Please tell me you're calling to let me know everything is okay and you didn't find a body."

"I wish I could, but Teresa Grant is dead," I confirm. "Dad and I came to check on her and found her hanging from her stairs just like I saw this morning." The sadness of that sentence settles on my heart.

"I'm so sorry," Ford says. "Send me the address and Tyler and I will be right there."

I hang up and text him the address, then lean back against the Cadillac to wait. "They're coming," I say to Dad.

"Good," he says. "Do you mind if we say a prayer for her?"

"Of course. That's a good idea." Dad takes both of my hands, and we bow our heads. He says a prayer for Teresa's soul and the sadness grows even deeper.

"I still can't quite believe this," I say when he finishes. "Who would want to murder an innocent old lady?"

"A monster." Dad leans back against the car next to me. "I almost hesitate to ask, because I truly hope she has already crossed into heaven, but do you sense her ghost anywhere nearby?"

I'm surprised I hadn't thought of this. I do a mental check of my back and there's a low tingle at the base of my spine. "I don't know. There's a tingle, but it's very faint."

"You don't see her anywhere?" He looks around the yard like he will be able to see her spirit himself.

"I don't. She did show me what happened and called out to me. That could have been before she crossed, though." I stand up straight. "Teresa? Are you out there?" I call.

The breeze picks up a bit and a bird twitters, but I don't see a ghost. "I'm sorry. I don't sense her," I say, feeling defeated.

"It was a long shot. Sure would be nice if she could tell you what happened."

"I say that all the time about my other cases, but it rarely works out that way." I sigh.

"So, this thing with your mom..." Dad begins, changing the subject. "You're not mad I called a family meeting yesterday, are you?"

"I think it was a good idea. At least everyone knows now. I'm glad the secret is out."

"Can I ask why it had to be a secret until now, though? You know Keaton should have been told at the very least." I don't like the slight note of recrimination in his voice, but I suppose I deserve it.

"I know, I know. I can't really explain it. You have to understand that at first, she wasn't herself. She was here, but not really here. It's only recently that she's been more like her whole self."

"That had to be hard."

"It was," I say simply.

"What are you going to do about her now? She can't stay on this side forever. It's not fair to her. Same goes for Elsa."

"When the time is right, I'll know and I'll help them." The thought makes my heart beat against my ribs. "Holy flip, I'm going to hate it, though. I'll be losing her all over again."

Dad places a hand on my shoulder. "We'll all be here with you. Plus, you have Ford now. You won't be alone."

"First, we have to find out who is behind all of this. I know it's all connected to the puppet, but I don't know why or how. So much death."

"And so much light." He grips my hand. "For all evil, there is a corresponding grace. You've been a blessing to so many souls."

"I appreciate that," I say. "But I'm tired. It's a lot of responsibility."

"Would you give your gift up if you could?"

It's a question that's floated through my mind at my weakest moments. I don't know the answer.

Luckily, I'm saved from having to give one because Ford's car pulls in to the gravel driveway.

He's not alone. Tyler climbs out of the passenger seat and the back door opens. Detective Faith Hudson has joined them.

She's been friendly enough to my face, but I get the distinct feeling she doesn't like me. I wish she hadn't come along. I'd rather deal with Ford and Tyler. At least they get me.

"She's inside," I say after we make our greetings and I introduce Dad to Faith.

Somberly, we enter the house and make our way down the hall to the living room. Faith breaks the silence first. "Okay, you're sure this isn't a suicide? It looks that way."

"It does at first glance, but look closely here." I point to the string marks above the rope. I glance at Ford in question.

"She knows about the puppet," he confirms.

I hide my surprise and continue. "I think these are from the puppet wrapping her in his strings. Look here where she clawed at them."

The three detectives look closely. "I see. You think the puppet did this to her?" Faith asks.

"I think he was part of it. He's not big enough to lift her up like this, so he had to have had help," I explain.

"Human help." Faith nods. To her credit, she seems to believe me. Or maybe she's just playing along.

"So we're looking for a deranged puppet that's helping murder old ladies?" Tyler says. "This morning is off to a wild start."

"Let's just focus on what's in front of us," Ford says. "What do you know about Teresa Grant?" he asks Dad.

"She has been a staple at the church for decades, teaching Sunday School, helping at dinners, that sort of thing. She lost her husband several years back and doesn't have any family here in Ashby."

"What about money?" Faith asks. "This is a modest house, but maybe she had money to inherit?"

"I doubt it," Dad says. "She and Gene lived simply. Besides, who would benefit? She only has a sister who lives in Florida. If the puppet is involved, then money isn't a motive. There has to be something else going on here."

"This has to be related to the other deaths," Ford says. "We need to stop this before anyone else gets hurt."

"But what would Teresa have to do with the puppet?" Tyler asks.

"Maybe it's just random?" Faith says.

"I think Holtzberry is on to something. There's a serial killer in town and now he's targeting innocent old ladies," Ford says.

"Who is Holtzberry?" Faith looks confused.

We all exchange looks.

"You all better tell me what's going on. I know about the puppet and the ghosts and things, but if there's another person involved, I should know," Faith says.

"Detective Jon Holtzberry used to be the head detective in Ashby," Ford starts to explain.

"So, he's retired?" Faith asks.

"He's dead. Most likely killed by whoever hurt Teresa."

Faith slowly pushes a thin braid behind her ear. "Let me guess, he's a ghost too and he's helping you."

I have to hand it to Faith, she doesn't miss much.

Before we can discuss further, we hear a car door closing. Tyler looks down the hall into the driveway. "Marrero's here," he says, the mood immediately sinking even further.

"I'd better go outside," I say. "He's not going to be happy to see me."

I look for a back exit, but Marrero comes in before I can sneak out. He stands in the entrance, his bag in hand, an angry expression on his face.

I brace for the retort, but he just shakes his head in disgust, then turns his attention to Teresa's body.

TWENTY-THREE
FORD PIERCE

I wait until Marrero has his back to Rylan, then motion for her to leave. She and Brett hurry out the door. I hate making her leave, but I don't want to tangle with the coroner over her presence.

I hope he'll not bring it up, but of course he does.

"That girl found another body?" Marrero comments, not turning from his preliminary inspection of Teresa.

"Yes, sir," I say, feeling defensive.

"How did she find this one? A ghost told her?" The sarcasm is heavy.

"Not exactly," I hedge. I don't want to tell him about Rylan's dream vision. That's a bit far out even for her.

Now he turns with intention and focuses his gray eyes on me. "It might help your career if you stayed away from her."

I bristle at the veiled threat. "My career is doing fine. What do you have against Rylan anyway?" I can't stop the words and they tumble out. "She has helped us in a lot of cases. Without her, poor Teresa would have been here for who knows how long. Rylan's gift is a blessing to our investigations, not a hindrance."

"You need her help to solve cases?" His eyes flash.

"I will use whatever tool will help me stop the killer, no matter how strange you think it is. I'm the detective on this case, I make the decisions." I know I'm pushing it. Until the coroner releases the scene, he is in charge.

"There is no case. This woman clearly did this to herself."

I want to point out the string marks on her neck, but I'd have to explain the puppet to the man. I know he won't like to hear about that.

"Are you sure?" I ask.

"I know all about you looking into that car crash from the other day. Are you making a habit out of second-guessing my findings? I've been at this job since you were in diapers."

I feel my face growing hot and I mentally tell myself to stay calm. It will not go well for me to get into a heated argument with him, especially after being called in to Chief McKay's office yesterday. "I'm not second-guessing. I just want to be sure."

Marrero picks up his bag that he brought in but never opened. "You can be sure of what I say."

Tyler and Faith have been listening all along but not intervening. I look to them for backup now.

"Are you absolutely certain she hung herself?" Tyler asks.

"It seems pretty obvious, doesn't it?" Marrero says. "Look around you. This woman clearly had a lonely life and spent her time doing puzzles. Maybe she just gave in."

He's right. There is a puzzle on a table nearby and several boxes of puzzles on the bookshelf next to books on grief and living alone. Brett said she didn't have any family really and gave her time to the church. Did she really just lose the battle with herself? We've seen it lots of times.

I look at the scratches on her neck and the faint lines above the rope. Maybe those aren't from the puppet, maybe she just changed her mind after she jumped and clawed at the rope.

It is a sobering thought.

"Always a pleasure, gentlemen," Marrero says to us as he heads out of the front door.

Rylan and her dad are standing by her car. A cruiser has pulled in behind her and Officer Frazier is now walking toward us. Behind him, Chief McKay's SUV pulls in.

This day just keeps getting better, I think sarcastically.

Frazier nods at Rylan and keeps walking. He joins a scene tech who is getting something out of the coroner's van.

Chief McKay stops short when he sees her, then looks at me and back at her.

"Hello, Chief," Rylan says sweetly.

He seems unimpressed. "I understand you found a body," he says, getting right to the point.

"I did."

"And you were with her?" he asks Brett.

"Yes. I knew Teresa."

McKay nods sagely, then says, "You can go. We can handle it from here."

"Don't you need our official statements?" Rylan asks.

"There is no need. It's clear what happened here," Marrero cuts in. "Suicide is a hard pill to swallow, but that's the unfortunate truth."

"Teresa would never have done that," Brett says, surprising all of us. "She was murdered."

"Mr. Flynn, I think it is best that you and your daughter leave now," McKay says.

Rylan looks like she's about to say something, her mouth opening then closing. Finally, she walks around the Cadillac and climbs in, visibly angry.

Once they are gone, McKay turns his ire on me. "Pierce, seriously, what did I say yesterday? Not everything is a murder investigation. I realize it's exciting to work cases with your girlfriend, but this has gone on long enough."

I don't like the way this is going, but hold my tongue for the chief.

Behind him, Frazier makes no effort to hide his smile.

"I am putting you on unpaid leave until further notice. Maybe a little more time off will remind you how this job works."

I can barely breathe. Leave?

"Chief, we really think Teresa Grant was murdered," Tyler jumps to my defense.

"Careful, or I will put you on leave too," McKay says. "I can't even trust my detectives to make rational decisions right now. I don't know what has gotten into you two lately, but all this Rylan Flynn ghost stuff has to end now. Understand?"

I'm shocked by how angry he is. I think about how Margie told me about the photo of McKay with Charlie Landry and how she thought maybe the chief was the killer we are all after. Is that why he's so mad, covering for his guilt?

I hate to think it, but it's starting to make sense.

"We understand," Tyler says. "But you don't know everything that is going on in this town."

"Don't bother," I mutter. "He wouldn't understand." Or would he? If he is in league with the puppet, I don't want him to know we are on to him.

"I think we are missing the point of why we are here," Marrero interrupts again. "That poor woman inside deserves our undivided attention, not bickering about Rylan Flynn."

This stops the conversation cold.

"Let's get her loaded into the van and clear this scene," McKay instructs. "Frazier, you stay and help. Detectives, you can go. We don't need you here. Pierce, I will continue this discussion at a later time."

No one argues with the chief. We all do as we are told, and I drive away with Tyler and Faith.

We don't say anything on the way back to Ashby, but my mind keeps repeating one thing.

This isn't over.

TWENTY-FOUR

Rylan was on the scene again. How did she know about Teresa? How does she find out everything?

I must stop her.

We must stop her.

I finally feel whole again now that Roland has returned.

Rylan can't ruin this for both of us.

TWENTY-FIVE
RYLAN FLYNN

I'm only too happy to leave Teresa's. I don't like being dismissed, but I prefer that to hanging around where I'm not wanted.

"For just once, I'd like them to say, 'thanks, Rylan'." I can't help the bitterness seeping out in my voice.

"That's never going to happen," Dad responds.

I hadn't meant to say that out loud and feel bad I'm complaining when Teresa is dead. "I'm sorry. I know this isn't about me. It's never about me. It's about the spirits."

"Just focus on that and you'll be fine," he says as I pull into his driveway.

"I appreciate you coming with me this morning," I say as I put the car in park. "I didn't want to find her alone. I know I've seen a lot of dead people, but it doesn't get any easier."

"It's not supposed to," he says sagely. "I'll check in with you later." He gives me a sideways hug and gets out of the car. I wait until he goes back inside, then pull out onto the street.

"I thought I'd never get you alone," Teresa Grant's ghost says from the passenger seat.

"Holy flip," I shout, startled.

"That's no way to talk," Teresa admonishes me.

"I'm sorry," I say contritely, feeling like a little girl in her presence.

"Keep driving and go out to Millburn Road," she says. "I want to show you something."

I dart my eyes at her neck, the rope and string marks easily visible. "What happened to you? Did the puppet try to strangle you?"

"This isn't the time to discuss that." She waves her hand.

"But who killed you?"

"I can't tell you. There is a lot you don't know, and I need to explain it all before you can find out the truth."

"Was it the same person that killed my mom?"

Teresa gives me a stern look. "Let me do this the way He wants me to. All will be revealed in due time."

"I don't like this."

"You think I like being dead?"

She has me there.

I follow her directions once we are on Millburn Road. "Turn here," she instructs.

The narrow dirt track next to a tree line is made for tractors, not big cars, but I do as she says. We bounce and jostle our way toward a stand of woods.

"Where are we going?" I ask, after my teeth jam together when we hit a big hole in the lane.

"Almost there."

Ahead, the late morning sun glints on what looks like a pond between the trees. A small gap in the woodland leads us to the water's edge.

"This looks sort of familiar," I say as I peer out of the windshield.

"Your dad used to take you here when you were a kid. It used to be a great fishing hole."

"And ice skating," I add, the memory rushing into my head. "Until the accident where I almost died and got my gift."

"Exactly," Teresa says. "Come with me."

Feeling like I'm in *A Christmas Carol*, following the Ghost of Christmas Past, I let Teresa lead me to the edge of the pond.

"It began long before you were born," she says as we look at the water. "Something bad came from this pond. Something bad that you've faced."

"The puppet," I say. "I thought it was Roland."

"It is, but what came from this pond turned the human Roland into the monster that he became. When he died, it was that monster that was locked in the puppet."

"And now he's running around killing innocent people like you."

"You and he are tied together."

I take a step away from the pond's edge. "I don't want to be tied to that horrible thing."

"For every evil, there is a light. You are the light."

A chill goes down my arms, making goosebumps raise. "I don't want that."

"Only God can decide, and He already did."

The wind picks up and lifts my hair, blowing it into my face. I tuck a strand behind an ear whilst reflecting deeply on Teresa's words. "Why did He choose me?" It's a question I've asked myself late at night many times. "I was just a kid at the time."

"I'm just here to tell you what happened. I can't tell you why He does what He does."

"Now what do I do?"

"You stop Roland and send him back where he came from." She points to the pond.

"I don't know where he is or how to catch him."

"You will."

"You sound like a fortune cookie," I say, growing angry. "I'm tired of all this mystery. Just tell me what to do."

The wind carries the sound of a child crying through the trees. Teresa looks in the direction it came from. "What is that?"

"It sounds like a kid," I say. "Why would a kid be out here?" I take several steps toward the crying.

Teresa follows me.

"Rylan, help."

It's Elsa. I'd recognize her anywhere.

I hurry into the trees, following her voice, fear coursing up my back.

On the other side of the trees is a farm with a big red bank barn and two silos. I stop. The farm looks familiar, but it seems no one is around.

"Rylan!" Elsa cries. I hurry past the silos toward the barn. The sliding doors are open a foot or so. I hear Elsa crying inside, so I shimmy through the gap.

The inside of the barn is quiet and dim. Light shines through the cracks in the wood, dappling the floor in sunlight. Each side of the space has a hayloft, and the center is open except for an orange tractor parked by the far wall. It smells like old manure.

"Elsa, what are you doing in here?" I call.

Her soft crying comes from the hayloft to the left. "Rylan, help, I'm stuck."

Without thinking, I climb the built-in wooden ladder.

Teresa suddenly appears in the loft above me. "Hurry," she says.

I reach the top of the ladder and climb onto the wooden planks above. The loft only holds a small stack of bales, and I can hear Elsa whimpering behind them.

I run around the bale stack and realize the floor is missing a section almost too late. I slide to a stop just before I fall through the hole.

Elsa's crying morphs into laughter I've heard too many times.

"Got ya," the puppet says and pushes me into the hole.

I land on one foot and feel my ankle crunch beneath me. The pain shoots up my leg, all the way to my hip. I scream and fall onto the concrete floor. I roll onto my side, reaching for my ankle. Above me, Roland looks through the hole, still laughing.

Teresa stands looking through the other side of the hole. "I'm so sorry, Rylan," she says. "It's for the best."

They move the missing piece of the hayloft floor back into place and I'm lost in darkness.

"Elsa!" I shout desperately.

"She's not here," Roland shouts. "Yeah, I'm not here," he says, mimicking her voice.

The pain in my leg nearly blocks out rational thought. Tears of frustration and pain roll down my cheeks. How could I be so stupid? Of course, Elsa isn't here.

How could Teresa have tricked me too?

Can't I trust anyone?

In my shock, the only eternally trustworthy thing comes to mind.

I lie on the cold concrete floor and pray.

TWENTY-SIX
RYLAN FLYNN

My prayers are short and to the point, and it doesn't take long until I'm once again distracted by the angry shooting pain of my ankle. It must be broken. Now that I've been in this dark place for a little while, my eyes have adjusted. Light filters through the hayloft floor above me.

Far above me.

Did I fall into the basement? Do barns have basements? I know bank barns do, the back open to the air like a walk-out basement, the front at ground level. The walls of this tiny room stretch up two floors to the loft, frustratingly smooth, with nowhere to climb even if I could.

I realize I can't even stand on two feet. I hobble around the space, searching for anything that might help me out of here. I find a narrow metal door and for a brief moment, I think I'm going to be okay.

The door doesn't move an inch. Either it is rusted in place, or it is locked on the outside.

Either way, I'm stuck here.

My phone isn't any help. No service in here, not even SOS service.

Nothing.

I slide down the concrete wall and put my head in my hands in despair. No one knows where I am. My car is basically hidden near the pond. No one will find it unless they know where to look.

And who would look?

Ford thinks I'm safe with Dad. Dad thinks I'm safe at home.

Even Mom and Holtzberry have no idea where I am. They don't even know about Teresa's death yet.

That leaves Elsa.

What could a little girl do to help me even if she wasn't a spirit?

The despair grows deeper. I've really gotten into a mess this time.

Time slides by and the painkillers I took this morning wear off. My stab wound begins to ache. That pain pales in comparison to the pain in my ankle.

It has swollen to almost twice the normal size. I untie my sneaker to make room, but the movement causes the broken bones to shift and stab.

I try to stay still, my back straight against the concrete wall.

What is this place?

In the corners, I notice some pieces of corn covered in dust. It must have been some sort of corn bin. Now it's a perfect cage.

But who owns it? I'm pretty sure this is the farm I saw across the street from Teresa's place. That doesn't get me anywhere, though. I don't know who her neighbors are or where our suspects live. What if it's not even any of the people we have been looking at?

So many questions and no way to get the answers.

I shift a little, my rear aching from the hard concrete. I need to get out of here.

"Roland?" I shout. "Where are you? Let me out."

I listen hard, but the walls block any sound I might hear.

Trying a different tactic, I call for Teresa. "Please help me," I beg.

After a long wait, she appears before me. "I'm not supposed to be talking to you," she says. "He doesn't want it to play out that way."

"You keep saying 'He' and I assume you mean God. Do you really think He wants me locked in here injured and hurting?"

"It's all part of the plan."

"What plan?!" I shout, losing my temper.

Teresa crouches before me and leans near my ear. "To get rid of what's inside Roland."

"How can I destroy the puppet from in here?"

"Not just the puppet, not even the ghost inside it. You need to destroy the evil inside that man's spirit."

"How?"

"You'll see. Please, just wait."

"I'm not good at waiting," I say.

"You really have no choice. I'm sorry." She disappears.

I call her name over and over, but she doesn't come back.

Time crawls by and I find myself dozing, occasionally jerking awake. I eventually give in and curl up on my side and wait.

And wait.

Until tiny footsteps cross the hayloft above me and the hatch I fell through suddenly opens.

TWENTY-SEVEN
ELSA WHITE

The house has been empty all day. I get that Ford had to go to work, but Rylan left without saying anything. Then Miss Margie and that Jon left, saying they wanted to go check in on his daughter, Brandie.

No one is checking on me.

No one even cares that I'm too young to be left alone all day, even if I'm dead already.

I try to fill the day with watching TV, but soon get bored with game shows and those icky soap operas that Miss Margie likes to watch.

I give up on the TV and wander around the house. There isn't much to wander around as it's still pretty full. I walk to the kitchen and wish I could have a cookie. I haven't had a cookie in a long time. Not that they would be very good even if I could. Rylan only has store-bought cookies, not the homemade ones like Mom always had on hand.

Once I got sick, I was allowed only one a day, but boy were they good.

I'm standing in the kitchen, staring at the closed cabinets when tears sneak up on me.

I miss Mom. I miss Dad.

I miss being alive.

Mostly, I miss being needed. I was the center of my parents' lives. Now I'm forgotten and left behind.

Maybe a visit home will do me good. There's nobody around to tell me I have to stay in this crowded house all day.

Focusing hard, I will myself into my old kitchen. Mom sits at the table, a can of Dr. Pepper in hand. This makes me smile. Mom always had a thing for Dr. Pepper. It was too sweet for me, but she loves it.

But despite having her favorite drink in hand, she looks sad.

"Mom, I'm here," I say gently.

To my surprise, she turns her head in my direction. It's probably a coincidence, but it makes my heart beat faster and gives me an idea. Something I'm surprised I haven't tried before.

"Mom," I say again, trying hard to make her hear me. "Mom, it's Elsa."

She stares right at me, and I almost feel she sees me.

I focus as hard as I've ever focused before. This is more important than moving boxes or opening doors.

"Mom, I'm here." A shiver travels up my legs and to my fingertips.

Mom sucks in a breath. "Oh, my God." She jumps up and spills the Dr. Pepper in the process. "Elsa? I see you."

I try harder, put all my strength into taking form for her.

She reaches out, but her hand passes right through me. She pulls her hand back as if she has been burned.

"How are you here?"

"I came to see you. I love you, Mom. I miss you."

"I miss you too. You have no idea how much I miss you. I think of you every day. Our lives have not been the same without you." Her voice breaks. "Are you okay? How does this work?"

"I'm as good as I can be. I'm staying with Rylan and the ghost of her mom. It's been nice."

"That woman told me you were still here as a ghost. But you should be in heaven!"

"I wanted to see you. And Dad. Is he here?"

"He's at work. Oh, Elsa. I... I just can't believe you're here."

"I'm getting tired, and I don't think I can stay much longer. Just know that I'm with you even when I'm not here. I'll always love you and someday I'll see you in heaven."

"Oh, baby. Don't go." She reaches for me again but still can't make contact. It almost hurts being so close but so far away.

"Goodbye, Mom. Tell Dad I love him," I manage before slipping into the ghost realm again.

"No, Elsa! Come back!" she screams into the kitchen. "Please don't leave again."

I summon my remaining energy and try to reappear, but I can't. I can only stand here and watch my mother cry for me.

It becomes too much and I have to leave. I don't give any thought to where I go, I just think "leave now."

When I open my eyes, I expect to be back at Rylan's house or even crossed into heaven now that I've been able to tell Mom goodbye. Instead, I'm in a barn, near a stack of hay bales in a loft.

"I knew you'd come," Roland says. "You're a good friend."

I know I shouldn't be here. Shouldn't be with the puppet.

But I stay.

TWENTY-EIGHT
FORD PIERCE

I drop Tyler and Faith off at the police station. I'm itching to go in with them and work on the cases that seem to have stacked up.

But I've been put on leave.

Leave!

This is different than the time off I took to care for Rylan. That I wanted to do. All I want to do now is solve these cases.

Rylan wouldn't let a little thing like being on leave stop her, though.

I just have to figure out where this all started. It didn't start with Margie. She most likely was killed because she knew something about Charlie Landry.

I have read the file on him. Basically, just a note in the system that he was shot in a hunting accident. "Mistaken for a deer," it said. "Shooter unknown."

That sounds fishy at best, even without Margie's story of a deathbed accusation.

There were other mysterious cases Holtzberry flagged as likely to involve the same killer, but I can't remember the addresses of any of these victims. I do remember Charlie Landry's, though.

I wonder if his widow is still there, and whether she will talk to me.

The two-story house is on the edge of town. A line of garden gnomes flanks the sidewalk. I feel like they are staring at me with suspicion as I make my way to the front door. "Leave her alone," they seem to say. "She's been through enough."

It's not the gnomes, it's my guilty conscience. I'm about to pick at what's sure to be a sore scab.

I knock on the green door and wait. Inside, a dog barks, but the door remains closed.

I knock again, this time louder.

It's entirely possible that Lynn Landry isn't home or maybe she even moved, but this is my only lead at the moment, so I knock a third time.

The door finally opens and a woman in a bath robe with wet hair looks out. "What?" she demands, holding a small dog back.

Not the friendliest of greetings, but I'll take it.

"Mrs. Landry?" I ask, flashing her my badge.

Her demeanor quickly changes and her shoulders slump. She positions herself so the door is between us and looks out. "I don't want to hear it. Not again. Please tell me Milo is okay."

I have no idea who Milo is. "He's fine. This is about Charlie."

Lynn's eyes narrow. "Charlie has been dead for two years. What could you possibly want with him now?"

"I just had a few loose ends I wanted to tie up," I start.

"Someone shot him while he was hunting. He died. What else can I tell you?" She steps onto the porch and faces me like she's ready to attack.

"I know that's what the official report says. I am just looking into a few other cases that might be related. I wondered if—"

"If I shot him?" she interrupts.

"I wasn't thinking that, but curious that you brought it up."

"I've lived under that suspicion all this time. Imagine what it's like to lose your husband and then have people whispering behind your back that they think you killed him. No one has come out and said it to my face, but I know what they are thinking. His parents won't even talk to me now. I was like a daughter to them, now I'm nothing. If it wasn't for Milo, I wouldn't have made it."

"Milo is your boyfriend, I take it?"

"Yes. You may know him. He's a crime scene tech."

"I don't know many techs, I'm afraid."

"He and Charlie were friends back in the day. Milo is one of the few people that tried to help after Charlie died. He's the only good thing to come out of this mess."

"I know this is hard, but I wondered if you have any ideas on who might have shot Charlie? Was there anyone who he had a disagreement with or who might want to hurt him?"

"Why are you asking this now? Can't you leave the dead in peace?" She tightens her robe over her chest.

"We think his death may be linked with others. I don't want to open old wounds, but if you do think of anything, please call me." I hand her a business card.

"There's nothing to think of. It was a freak accident." She sounds like she desperately wants to believe that. She fully opens the front door and the little dog runs out, yapping at my heels. She makes no move to stop the dog and closes the door, leaving me alone with the animal.

"Okay, buddy," I say to the dog as I return to my car. It follows a few paces but stops near the gnomes. It keeps barking as I pull out onto the street.

As I drive toward Rylan's, I realize that this Milo might also have access to the police computer system.

I call Tyler. "I think we need to look into Lynn Landry and her boyfriend, Milo. I don't have his last name, but he works for Marrero." I tell him a little more about my visit with the widow.

"Michelle will know who he is," Tyler reassures me.

"I would look into it, but..."

"Yeah, I wouldn't get too close to this after what McKay said this morning."

"I'll do what I need to do to stop this monster."

"I'm right here with you. Just don't get caught."

I finish with Tyler and drive the last few blocks to Rylan's house. The only bonus of being put on leave is that I get to spend some more time with her. I want to make sure she's okay after the way Marrero and McKay treated her this morning.

I'm surprised her car isn't in the driveway when I pull in next to her usual spot. Maybe she's still with her dad? That's a logical conclusion, but a niggle of worry starts low in my belly.

Wherever she is, I hope she isn't getting herself into trouble. It's happened too many times in the recent past.

I let myself into the house. Onyx runs up to me, meowing loudly to be fed.

Absently, I pour food into his bowl and make sure he has fresh water. All the time, I'm wondering if I'm alone or if it just feels like that. Living with ghosts you can't see is a bit unsettling. It's not so bad when Rylan is here to tell me what's going on, but this is the first time I've been in the house without her since finding out about her mom.

"Margie? Elsa?" I call, feeling foolish. "Holtzberry?" I add.

Of course, there isn't a response. Did I really think there would be?

I find a beer in the fridge, crack it open and take a long drink. As long as Rylan is busy, I can be busy too. There are only a few things left in the dining room and then it will be totally cleared. I might as well do something while I wait for her to get home.

Two faces look down at me from the hatch. I'm shocked to see Elsa. Although, is it really Elsa or some hallucination Roland is creating in my mind? He can mimic her voice believably, so can he make me think I'm seeing her too?

"Rylan, why are you down there?" she asks. Either I hit my head and this is all in my mind or Elsa really is here.

"Elsa, you have to get me out of here. Stay away from the puppet."

"He's my friend," she says. "He wants me. You all left me again."

"I'm so sorry, Elsa, but you can't help him. He's evil."

"You and your evil talk," she says. "Why won't you leave him alone?"

I can hardly believe the words I'm hearing. "He helped kill a woman last night. Teresa Grant died because of Roland and whoever he has under his control now."

Elsa shrugs. "I don't know anything about that." Is there a waver of uncertainty in her voice?

"There's a door down here. It's locked from the outside.

Come down here and unlock it and let me out." I try to stand on my broken ankle.

"Stop talking to her," Roland snaps. "You don't have any say here."

"Elsa, I'm hurt. You have to help me," I beg.

"I can't help you," she says.

Roland turns away and I hear the hatch sliding across the loft. Elsa takes the moment to put her finger to her lips in a shush motion and to wink at me before I'm in darkness again.

What did she mean by that? Was she trying to tell me she's still on my side? That makes sense. Elsa is sweet and innocent. There is no way she would hurt me on purpose.

Except whatever is in Roland is strong. It feels like the same power has been in all the killers I've stopped.

Is Elsa strong enough to resist it?

I sink back to the floor and stare at a crack on the opposite wall. The faint light coming through the gaps in the loft is beginning to fade.

I'm hungry and thirsty and need a restroom.

I do what I need to in a corner of the room and sit back down on the cold concrete. Panic begins to gnaw at the edges of my mind. Will I ever be found? Ford must have noticed I'm gone by now. Mom must be worried, not that she could tell anyone.

I keep watching the crack and trying to ignore the deep ache in my ankle. A spider wanders across the wall toward the crack. I keep an eye on it as it climbs up and down the wall.

"The itsy, bitsy spider climbed up the waterspout," I start to sing under my breath.

Soon, I'm singing loudly. Who cares? There's no one around to hear me.

My voice fades away and I sit in the growing darkness. Now that I'm not singing, the panic begins to bubble again.

What does the puppet want with me?

If Teresa is right and we are connected, the light and the dark, I can only imagine he wants me gone. But why hold me captive and not just kill me?

I don't want to explore that question too far.

Instead, I close my eyes, tip my head back against the wall and think about Ford. He has to be looking for me. He has to find me. He has always come when things looked desperate. This can't be how my life ends. Not here in this old corn bin.

I sense I'm not alone and open my eyes. Elsa stands before me.

"Are you okay?" she asks.

"What are you doing here? It isn't safe for you to be working with Roland."

"I'm not actually with him. I'm just pretending so I can help you."

"That's too dangerous. If you really want to help, you'll go home. I can't worry about you and me at the same time."

She stomps a small foot. "Everyone just wants to leave me out of things. I can help and I will."

"How?"

"I don't know yet. I do know that Roland is keeping you as a gift to the man that owns the farm."

Excitement courses through my veins. "Did he say his name?"

"No, but Roland is getting excited. I think he'll be home soon."

"Elsa, come back," Teresa calls from somewhere inside the barn.

Elsa looks torn. "I have to go. I'm sorry, but it will all be okay soon. Teresa says it's all part of the plan."

I'm tired of hearing of a plan that no one will explain to me.

Elsa disappears, and when I look again, the spider has disappeared too.

THIRTY
MARGIE FLYNN

When Jon asks me to come along with him to visit his daughter, Brandie, I jump at the chance. When we were alive, I saw photos of the twelve-year-old, but I never met her. He talked of her so often, I felt I knew her, though.

Now, as we hold hands and he focuses on her, a tiny frisson of fear enters my heart. It's normal to be nervous, I tell myself. I don't have long to think about it, as we soon are with Brandie.

She sits on a patio chair in her backyard, earbuds in and scrolling her phone. The two years that have passed have brought obvious changes to the girl from the photographs. She's almost a young woman now, fresh and pretty.

Jon sucks in a breath when he sees her. "She's really growing up," he says. "I visited her when I first realized I was a spirit and could travel, but it hurt too much to come back again."

"Well, you're here now."

"That's because I wanted you to meet her, at least in our fashion."

I feel awkward standing here watching the girl when she doesn't know. There isn't much to watch. She just bobs her head a little to whatever music she listens to and runs her thumb over her phone screen, pausing now and again to look at something.

"I wish I could talk to her," Jon whispers.

"Talk," I say. "She won't hear you, but it will make you feel better."

He rubs his mustache nervously. "I'm not sure what to say."

"Do you want me to give you some space?"

"No. I want you here." He studies Brandie, then says, "Hey, kid. It's Dad."

Brandie keeps bobbing her head to the music in her earbuds.

"I, um, I wanted to introduce you to the woman I love, Margie. She's right here. I'm sorry you didn't get to know her when we were alive."

Brandie's thumb pauses and she lifts her head from her phone to look out over the backyard.

"Do you think she hears me?" Jon asks, full of hope.

"She might sense something. Keep talking."

"You're really growing up. I'm so sorry I haven't been here to see it. I would give anything to change that."

Brandie takes out an earbud and rubs her upper lip the way her dad does. She seems to notice the motion and freezes, her eyes wide.

"Dad?" she whispers.

"I'm here, baby. I'm here," Jon yells.

The patio door opens and a woman steps out. "Lunch is ready."

"That's her mom," Jon says. "Of course she had to ruin this. Brandie, don't go. Please, don't go."

Brandie slides her phone into the back pocket of her jeans and heads for the door. She stops before stepping in and faces the yard. "I miss you, Dad," she whispers, then goes inside.

Jon beams with excitement. "She knew I was here. She knew."

"I think she did. That's so wonderful," I say.

He takes me into his arms. "Thank you for this. I'm so glad you got to see her. She's something, isn't she?"

"She's great. She is just lovely."

"You two would have really gotten along. Just think, if things had worked out differently, Rylan and Keaton would have a little sister."

"Yeah, differently..." I run a hand over the hole behind my ear. He sees the movement and is instantly sobered. I feel bad I ruined the mood.

"We will find out who did this to us," he says with conviction. "Let's go see what the chief is up to. Maybe he'll let something slip."

We hold hands again and focus on the chief. We arrive at his office just as he taps something into his computer. Jon skirts around the desk and looks at the screen. "Doesn't look important. Just some vandalism case from a few days ago."

"Does the chief usually handle vandalism cases?" I ask.

"Not usually." He bends toward the screen. "Just what I thought, Frazier was the one to answer the call. Frazier, McKay, I can't decide which one it might be."

I wander around the office while he studies the computer screen. I end up looking at the framed hunting picture I saw last time. McKay, Charlie Landry and another man pose for the camera. I bend to look closer.

"What you got?" Jon asks. "We already looked at that. It's the chief, Charlie Landry and some guy I've seen around the crime scenes. Milo something."

"Do you think he could be involved? This Milo guy?"

"He hasn't come up. I suppose he would have access to the computer system, the same as the other suspects. What are you thinking?"

"I'm not sure. Maybe he went hunting with Charlie and shot him."

"And then shot you and then gave me something to make it look like I had a heart attack. I mean it could be that. I still think McKay or Frazier had better motives."

"Serial killers don't need motives. They just need to kill," I say.

"Good point."

I look at the picture again, sure it means something. "We're forgetting one thing." I say, realization dawning. "There are actually four people in this group."

"What do you mean?" Jon asks.

"Who's the person taking the photo?"

"This is getting us nowhere." Jon sighs.

We've now been watching McKay most of the day, but he hasn't done anything remotely suspicious. We even followed Frazier for a while when he was at the station, but he just did normal police work. Nothing tied to our murders.

Later in the day, we do learn something. It seems Rylan found Teresa Grant, the old Sunday School teacher, hanging from her stairs this morning. An officer is talking about it with a black detective with long braids. This must be the new detective Rylan was telling me about, Faith Hudson.

"Trouble follows that girl all over town," the uniformed officer says.

"She's just trying to help. There's a lot going on around here that you don't know," Faith says.

"Like ghosts? What a load of crap. When I make detective, you can bet I won't let that woman around my cases."

"Rylan has a lot to offer," Faith says. "Without her, that woman would still be hanging all alone."

"Or she might be alive," the officer retorts, then walks away.

The conversation rattles me. Is this what people really say

about my baby girl? Don't they realize all she's done for this town?

"Let's go home," I say to Jon. "I want to see Rylan."

We reappear in my bedroom. I expect to see Elsa on the bed watching TV, but she's not here. I feel a stab of guilt. We've been gone much longer than I expected. It's growing dark outside. I should not have left Elsa alone all day.

I try and console myself with the thought that she'd have had Rylan with her.

I leave Jon in the room and go to look for my daughter. I find Ford alone in the front room, moving boxes around. He stops and checks his phone, his face tight. He taps out a quick message, then goes back to work, but he's obviously preoccupied.

Rylan is not with him. Thinking she's lying down for a rest, I check her room. Onyx is on her bed, but Rylan is not there.

Worry wriggles up my spine. No Elsa. No Rylan. What can that mean?

I go back to Ford, wishing I could ask him what he knows. Judging by the way he checks his phone again, I can tell he's worried too.

This can't be good.

"Okay, I give in," Ford mutters to himself and places a call. "Hey, Brett. Is Rylan with you?" he asks.

He listens for a moment as I hold my breath, then says, "That's what I thought. She's been gone all day and isn't answering her phone or texts." Ford listens to Brett's response. "I think I'll try Mickey. Maybe she's over there."

I watch him talk to Mickey with the same result. Rylan isn't with her.

The wriggle of worry blooms into full panic.

Rylan is missing and I'm sure *he* has her.

I just don't know who he is.

Ford's phone rings and he answers it quickly. "Rylan?" His

face falls. It's not Rylan. "Yes, this is Detective Pierce," he says politely. "What can I do for you, Mrs. Landry?" He walks into the kitchen, puts the phone on speaker and sets it on the counter as he gets a drink of water.

"You told me to call if I thought of anything," the woman who must be Charlie Landry's widow says. "I'm sure it's nothing, but it keeps popping into my mind..."

Ford sets down the glass, his attention now fully captured. "What did you think of?"

"Back in the weeks before Charlie was killed, he had a new hunting buddy. He hunted with a lot of people in the police department and such. Milo got him into the group. I didn't think it mattered at the time since it was an accident, but if you think there's more to it... well, I don't know."

"Lynn, who are you suspecting?" He grabs the phone and holds it tight.

"I don't want to spread gossip or anything like that, but this man used to give me the creeps."

Jon joins me in the kitchen as Ford starts to lose patience. "Who? Please tell me."

She says a name.

A name I never thought would come up in this investigation but now makes perfect sense.

The panic pounds through me.

We have to find Rylan and fast.

THIRTY-ONE
RYLAN FLYNN

When the hatch opens again, I can barely make out the face looking down at me. There's a light bulb behind him in the loft, throwing his face into shadow.

Once I realize who it is, I think I'm saved.

Then the puppet appears next to him. "You did good, Roland," Marrero says. "Real good."

Marrero.

Shock makes me go cold.

I thought he was just a grumpy old man, but he's a killer.

He killed Mom and who knows how many others.

I jump to my feet, forgetting about my ankle until it screams with pain.

"How can you do this?" I shout. "You killed my mom."

"Oh, Rylan. Why don't you just ask the ghosts like you always do? I'm sure they have all the answers." His voice is dark and menacing. How did I never notice that before? I guess because I spent all my time trying to avoid him.

"I want my answers from you," I practically spit.

"You don't deserve answers," Marrero shouts down at me. "But I've waited for this day for a long time. Ever since I realized what you are. Roland explained it to me." He puts a hand on Roland's back, a gentle gesture that seems so out of place. "I do appreciate you keeping him safe all these years. I missed him."

"How do you know about Roland?"

Marrero shifts until he's sitting on the edge of the hatch, his feet dangling. I wish he was closer so I could grab him and pull him into the corn bin.

"Roland and I go way back," he says like he's telling me a bedtime story. "I saw him at an auction and was drawn to him. I was only a kid, but my parents let me bid on him. I was the highest bidder and he was mine." He looks at Roland fondly as the puppet continues to grin down at me. "I realized early on that he was special. It was like he could read my mind. When he started talking, I was scared at first, but then I learned to trust him. Trust the things he told me to do."

"That was the evil in him," I say.

"Evil is just the way you look at it. I don't see it that way. I see it as my true calling. I've always been fascinated by death. That's why I went to medical school and became a coroner. I could feed my need for death without having to cross the line."

"The line to being a killer. When did that start?"

"When I realized I could write off bodies as accidents or natural causes. Coroners have a lot of power. No one second-guesses them. I could do what I wanted, and no one was any the wiser. I just had to be creative in my methods."

His words are making me sick, but I try to keep him talking. "But you got rid of the puppet. Keaton found it in the dump."

"That wasn't my fault. My first wife had an inkling that something wasn't right with Roland and with me. She threw him in the trash, and he was gone before I could get him back." Marrero laughs. "Don't worry, I got rid of her too. That was one of my favorites."

"You killed your wife?"

"Haven't you been listening? She slipped in the shower and hit her head. Happens all the time."

I feel sick listening to him talk of murder so callously. "You won't get away with this," I say.

"Rylan dear, no one will stop me." He smacks his knees. "Now, let's get this show on the road. I could sit here all night and reminisce about old times, but I'd rather get to the true reason you're here."

"Wait," I say. "I need to know. Why did you kill Mom?"

"Your silly mom. She and Holtzberry thought no one knew about their relationship. What a joke. As soon as Holtzberry started poking around Charlie Landry, I knew where he got the information. That's the only time I even got close to being caught."

"So, then you killed Holtzberry too. Faked a heart attack like you did with Jacob McClure."

"Such a busy body," Marrero says. "You've been doing your research. That McClure, I did him on a whim. He cut me off at the pump the day before and I was bored. I put something in his coffee at the gas station and you know the rest. I never imagined it would be you and Pierce who would be involved when he crashed his car. I laughed all the way back to the morgue."

"You know, I never liked you, but you really are sick."

Marrero and the puppet laugh almost in unison. "You'll see how sick I am," Marrero says. Then he shuts the hatch, closing me back into darkness once again.

"Don't worry," Elsa whispers. "I'm still here with you."

"I'm here too," Teresa says.

"I don't want you here. It's your fault I'm in this mess," I hiss at Teresa. "And don't you give me any story about God wanting this."

"Some things are bigger than you," Teresa says.

If she wasn't a ghost, I'd slap her.

The metal door leading into the corn bin creaks open. I

push against it and try to make a run for it, but my swollen ankle stops me. So do the hands grabbing me by the arms.

"Nice try," Marrero says, cranking my arms behind my back. I feel thin plastic entwine my wrists and tighten. I pull until the zip ties cut into my skin, but they hold.

Marrero pushes me into a waiting wheelbarrow, and I land on my back, on top of my hands. I kick, but that makes my ankle scream again.

"You might as well stay still. It's a short ride to the pond. Just enjoy it," Roland says, walking along next to me.

"Why the pond?" I ask.

"All of this started at the pond," Marrero says. "That's where you got your gift. That's where you'll give it to me."

"I don't understand," I say, squirming in the wheelbarrow bumping along the lane leading back to the pond.

"You don't need to understand, you just need to die," Marrero says, his sinister tone heavy. "I'm going to enjoy this."

We reach the pond edge, and he dumps me out of the wheelbarrow onto the ground next to a rope, a knife, a syringe, a hammer and a gun.

"What are you going to do to me?" I whimper, panicked, lying on my side in the grass, the rope near my nose.

"Everything," Marrero says, rubbing his hands together. "What do you want to start with?" he asks the puppet.

Lynn Landry says the name Henry Marrero and everything clicks into place. Of course he's the killer. He could say cause of death was whatever he wanted on an autopsy report, or even say that an autopsy wasn't needed. He claimed Holtzberry was a heart attack as well as Jacob McClure. He said Charlie Landry was a hunting accident. More likely he was hunted.

My mind reels with all the implications and connections. How did we miss Marrero? He'd hated Rylan all along. That should have been my first clue that he was bad.

Now he may have Rylan.

I don't want to jump to conclusions, but it's too coincidental that she's missing and he just killed Teresa last night. And played it off as a suicide. What a monster.

Could he be in with the puppet, too, since there were string marks on Teresa?

I have to find Rylan and bring her home. No telling what Marrero and the puppet will do to her.

I call Tyler and tell him what I've found out. He does a quick computer search and gives me Marrero's address. Right across the street from Teresa Grant's.

This has to be where Rylan is.

At a run, I leave the house making sure I have my gun on my hip.

Marrero's house is dark when I pull into the driveway. My headlights shine on the huge red barn, the door open a few feet. I sit in my car all keyed up but not sure what to do now.

If Rylan is here, where would he keep her?

This looks like a peaceful farm. The barn sits on a bank attached to a pasture where animals might have once roamed. Silos stretch to the sky, bright in the full moon.

I climb out of my car, my nerves on edge and my senses alert.

"Rylan?" I yell across the dark farm.

Would she be in the house or the barn or the wood behind?

The house is dark, not a window lit. The barn has a light on, so I decide to check there first.

I turn sideways and slip through the opening between the sliding doors. Once inside, way up above the haylofts, two bulbs, one on each side, give a little glow to the open space. An orange tractor sits between the lofts.

"Rylan?" I call out into the dim. "Are you here?"

In the corner, by the tractor something begins to glow. I squint my eyes as I see the image of a little girl beginning to form.

"Elsa?" I gasp.

"She's by the pond out back," Elsa says. "You can't go, though, she has something to do."

I don't answer or ask questions, I just run from the barn, this time with my gun in hand.

THIRTY-THREE

RYLAN FLYNN

Marrero pulls me to a sitting position, my hands still tight behind my back. I look around and see Teresa watching the activity. Across the pond, Mom and Holtzberry appear.

"Mom, help!" I scream.

"Oh, so there are ghosts here." Marrero chuckles softly to himself. "They won't help you."

"Just kill her," Roland snarls. "Stop playing around."

"I need her to give me her powers first."

"I'll never do that," I say. "Never."

"That's what these are for." He picks up the knife and holds it to my throat. The point pricks my skin.

"You'll have to do better than that," I spit at him. "I've already been stabbed and I survived."

"I know. I was so hopeful that I was going to sign your death certificate then, but you lived. Too bad."

"Sorry to disappoint you."

Mom rushes Marrero and tries to stop his hand, but he slides the knife along my jaw line. The slice stings, but it's not too deep. "Leave her alone!" Mom screams.

"You know," Marrero says conversationally, "my least

favorite killing was your mom. I don't like guns, they are messy and leave all kinds of questions that police look for answers to. You should thank me I only shot her. I could have cut her throat too."

"I won't thank you for anything," I say, feeling the blood drip slowly down my neck.

"Just kill her already," Roland repeats.

"Leave her be," Mom screams, but he can't hear her.

"The doors are opening," Teresa says. Her voice is quiet, but it grabs my attention.

Next to the pond, two glowing doorways have appeared. One is bright, the door I've seen to Heaven many times. The other, I've never seen. It has a green light. The same light I've seen emanating from the cursed objects all the recent killers have been linked to.

The door to hell.

Marrero is momentarily transfixed by the doors. I'm surprised he can see them. "Now give your powers to me," he hisses. "I want to talk to the dead!"

"Never."

He tosses the knife on the ground. "This is too impersonal. I want you to beg me. To beg for your life." He pushes me back on the grass and straddles my chest. His hands clamp around my neck, sliding in my blood. I can smell the fishy scent of the pond and feel the mud squish into my hair.

Then all I can focus on is the fingers around my throat and my need for air.

"Do it. Do it!" Roland shouts.

Mom beats at Marrero's back and Holtzberry tries to kick him. They pass right through him.

"Just keep fighting," Teresa says. "It's almost over."

My vision turns dark. I've almost drowned before, but this is worse. I am so close to air, I just have to open my mouth and breathe in. I desperately try this, but no air enters my lungs.

The hands on my throat tighten. "Give them to me!" Marrero screams.

I'm so close to giving in. Can I give him my powers? This is where it all started, after all. Is this where it ends?

My eyelids flutter and I begin to lose consciousness. I should just give them to him. I can live without my gift.

A gunshot rings across the clearing and Marrero collapses across me. His hands slip away from my neck as he falls and I gasp hungrily. The dead man's body is heavy, and I scramble out from under him as best I can.

"Ford," Mom shouts.

I rub my sore and bloodied neck and look for the man I love.

Ford runs to me, takes me in his arms. "Oh my God, are you okay?" he asks, touching my face, touching my hair.

I sink into him. He realizes my hands are bound and grabs the knife with my blood on the tip and cuts the zip ties. I throw my arms around him.

"We thought we lost you," Elsa says.

"Rylan, are you okay?" Mom asks.

"This isn't over," Teresa says. "The doors are still open."

I suddenly know what I need to do.

"Where is Roland?" I ask, pushing myself to my feet. Too late, I remember my broken ankle. I hop on one foot and look around the clearing, which is still lit by the doors.

Suddenly, the puppet jumps from a nearby tree and bowls me over. We roll across the grass toward the green door.

He stands and pulls my arm toward the light.

"Leave me alone!" I scream, but he keeps pulling.

The green light envelops me and a horrible sick feeling permeates my soul.

"Come with me," Roland hisses.

"Never." A hot wind blows against my face, tosses my hair. I'm slipping into the green, the door to my world growing smaller. "Let me go." I shake him off and reach for the real world.

A hand reaches for mine, clamps me tight, and pulls.

Roland grips my ankles, pulling me down to hell. I kick hard, not caring that it hurts. His hold breaks and the hand pulling me out drags me back to the pond.

Mom and I tumble onto the grass, breathing hard.

Almost too late, I notice Roland crawling out of the door toward me. I grab the hammer that lies next to Marrero's dead body and swing it at the puppet. "Die, you miserable thing!" I smash the hammer into the jester's blue-star-painted eyes, shattering his face. I keep smashing until the puppet lies in splinters.

A horrible green light raises up and hovers slightly above the wrecked wood and strings: Roland's true self, the ghost that has embodied the puppet for nearly a century.

"Don't send me there," the spirit begs. "I don't want to go."

"Then you shouldn't have killed your wife," I say and kick with my good foot. Roland's ghost tumbles into the green door.

The door glows bright, then shuts suddenly, leaving just the white light door and a peace I haven't felt in a long time.

"It's time," Teresa says. "You did what He needed you to do." She moves to the doorway and reaches her hand for Mom and Holtzberry. "It's time for you too. He's been waiting."

Mom looks at me, afraid. "I don't want to leave you."

"It's okay, Mom. You will always be with me, even in heaven. You and Jon deserve your happily ever after." These feel like the hardest words I've ever had to say.

Mom begins to cry, but takes Jon's hand. She locks eyes with me as she steps into the light. "I love you, Rylan."

She's gone.

Really gone.

The grief tears into my heart.

I search for Ford. He stands just behind me and takes my hand.

The door closes and the pond clearing is now bathed only by the light of the full moon. Marrero lies on the grass, the remnants of the puppet next to him.

"I see the doors are gone," Ford says. "Does that mean the ghosts are gone too?"

I think for a long moment, then say, "So are my powers."

The only lie I ever tell him.

THIRTY-FOUR
RYLAN FLYNN

One Year Later

My feet hurt, especially my ankle that I broke a year ago. My shift at Aunt Val's donut shop is almost over. Soon I can go home to Ford and sit on the couch.

The thought makes me happy and also makes me sad. My house is no longer full of stuff. We cleaned it out soon after the showdown with Marrero. Ford has moved in, and I couldn't be happier.

I look at the ring on my finger. Even though I've worn the diamond for three months and seventeen days, it still feels like I'm living a dream.

Mrs. Rylan Pierce.

I like the sound of that.

Just a few months more and that will be my name.

The front door of the shop opens and I look up.

A huge smile crosses my face. Mickey comes in with a stroller holding baby Opal. She doesn't get out much since she had the baby. This visit is a rare treat.

I turn the sign on the door to 'closed' and settle us into a booth.

"You look good," I say. "Motherhood is your true calling."

Mickey takes Opal from the stroller and hands her to me. The little bundle of wriggles settles into my arms. I touch my lips to my god-daughter's head.

"I love being a mom. You should try it," Mickey says with a smile.

"Married first," I say. "Just a few months away."

"I'm so excited for you," Mickey practically squeals. She takes a sip of the coffee I've put in front of us. "But I wonder sometimes... do you miss it?"

I know what *it* is.

"I don't miss seeing ghosts. My life is so much simpler now. I get to help Val with this store so she can focus on the other new location. I go home to Ford. I've even started teaching Sunday School at Dad's church."

She takes another sip of her coffee, looking at me over the rim of the paper cup. "I'm glad for you," she says.

But I feel my best friend wants to say something else.

"I really don't miss the ghosts at all," I say with as much conviction as I can.

Does she know I'm lying?

We have a nice visit and talk of regular things, not murder. Mostly, I stare at Opal, fascinated by her dark hair and tiny features. I can't help wondering what Ford's baby will look like.

Someday.

When I'm ready.

All too soon, Mickey says she has to get back. I return Opal to the stroller and hold Mickey tight.

"I miss you." The words slip out.

"I miss you too. But I'll see you at Keaton's wedding in two weeks."

Keaton's wedding. An event I have mixed feelings about. Cheryl still doesn't seem to like me, and Keaton has been even more distant after he found out about me hiding Mom's ghost from him. Still, I wish my brother well.

"In two weeks," I repeat and release my best friend.

I lock the door behind her, close the shop down properly and head home. Ford is still at work. Although the body count is down in Ashby these days, there is still plenty for a detective to do.

I let myself into the front door of my cleared house.

"Elsa, are you here?" I call into the strangely uncluttered space.

"Are we finally alone?" she asks, coming into the living room with a book. "Can you read some *Little House* to me?"

A LETTER FROM DAWN

Dear reader,

I want to say a huge thank you for choosing to read *The Last Haunting* If you did enjoy it, and want to keep up to date with all my latest releases, just sign up at the following link. Your email address will never be shared and you can unsubscribe at any time.

www.secondskybooks.com/dawn-merriman

I hope you loved *The Last Haunting* and if you did I would be very grateful if you could write a review. I'd love to hear what you think, and it makes such a difference helping new readers to discover one of my books for the first time.
time.
I love hearing from my readers and I interact on my Fan Club on Facebook at the link below. Join the club today and get behind-the-scenes info on my works, fun games and interesting tidbits from my life.

www.facebook.com/groups/dawnmerrimannovelistfanclub

Again, thank you for reading *The Last Haunting*.

Happy reading and God bless,

Dawn Merriman

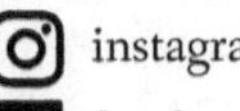 instagram.com/dawnmerrimannovelist
facebook.com/dawnmerrimannovelist

ACKNOWLEDGMENTS

Wow, Rylan has been on quite a ride! She has been so much fun to write. I feel honored to have brought you seven books of her adventures. I hope you all have loved her like I have. I will miss her now that her story is completed, but I'm glad she finally got her happily ever after. I wish her and Ford all the joy they deserve.

It takes a team to make these books come true. First and always, I thank my husband, Kevin. His unwavering support gets me through the days when the words won't come. Brainstorming sessions with him are sure to spark an idea that I then write into the story. Without him, I would not have been able to follow my dream of becoming an author. Thank you, Kevin.

To my beta readers, Carlie Frech, Jamie Miller, Candy Wajer and Katie Hoffman, your insights on all the Rylan books have been invaluable. Thank you for taking the time to read the rough pages. Thank you for talking me through the sticky spots and listening when I need to "talk books." I appreciate each of you. A special thank you to Chase Frech for talking plot lines with me.

A huge thank you to Bookouture and Second Sky Books and the wonderful team there. A special thank you to my editor, Jack Renninson. You took a chance on my little ghost hunter mystery stories, and I am so glad you did. It has been an honor and a privilege to work with you.

A writer is nothing without readers. Thank you to everyone who has stuck with Rylan through all her books. I am humbled by the following Rylan has, and it is because of you all. Happy reading.

The biggest thank you of all goes to God. All of this is through Him.

God Bless,

Dawn Merriman

PUBLISHING TEAM

Turning a manuscript into a book requires the efforts of many people. The publishing team at Bookouture would like to acknowledge everyone who contributed to this publication.

Audio
Alba Proko
Sinead O'Connor
Melissa Tran

Commercial
Lauren Morrissette
Hannah Richmond
Imogen Allport

Cover design
Damonza.com

Data and analysis
Mark Alder
Mohamed Bussuri

Editorial
Jack Renninson
Melissa Tran

Copyeditor
Lusana Taylor-Khan

Proofreader
Catherine Lenderi

Marketing
Alex Crow
Melanie Price
Occy Carr
Cíara Rosney
Martyna Młynarska

Operations and distribution
Marina Valles
Stephanie Straub
Joe Morris

Production
Hannah Snetsinger
Mandy Kullar
Ria Clare
Nadia Michael

Publicity
Kim Nash
Noelle Holten
Jess Readett
Sarah Hardy

Rights and contracts
Peta Nightingale
Richard King
Saidah Graham

Dear Reader,

We'd love your attention for one more page to tell you about the crisis in children's reading, and what we can all do.

Studies have shown that reading for fun is the **single biggest predictor of a child's future life chances** – more than family circumstance, parents' educational background or income. It improves academic results, mental health, wealth, communication skills, ambition and happiness.

The number of children reading for fun is in rapid decline. Young people have a lot of competition for their time, and a worryingly high number do not have a single book at home.

Hachette works extensively with schools, libraries and literacy charities, but here are some ways we can all raise more readers:

- Reading to children for just 10 minutes a day makes a difference
- Don't give up if children aren't regular readers – there will be books for them!

- Visit bookshops and libraries to get recommendations
- Encourage them to listen to audiobooks
- Support school libraries
- Give books as gifts

There's a lot more information about how to encourage children to read on our websites: **www.RaisingReaders.co.uk** and **www.JoinRaisingReaders.com**.

Thank you for reading.